twin sister's. It's a very good likeness of Anna," Ian murmured.

Bailey nodded. "And of you."

He lifted his gaze toward her, his dark eyes flaming so intently she could almost feel the heat. "I didn't know how to tell you."

A flicker of anger started to penetrate the numbing shock that held Bailey in its grasp. "I see. So you left me in ignorance. You lied to me." She lifted an unsteady hand to her aching temple. "God, I feel like Lois Lane."

Ian frowned. "Who?"

"Another woman too stupid to put two and two together."

"You aren't stupid. Far from it."

"Funny," she said with a flat laugh. "I'm feeling pretty dense. I came here to escape the mess I'd made of my life in Chicago, and now look what I've done. I've fallen for a ghost."

"Ever since I first came up with ideas for my 'Wish' books, I've been anxious to write Ian's story," confides **Gina Wilkins**. "There was something special about Ian. He was always so responsible, so brooding, so...lonely. I knew he needed an exceptional woman. But like the gentleman he is, Ian insisted his sister, Anna, find happiness first in *A Valentine Wish*. I hope you find Ian's story worth the wait."

A Wish for Love is Gina's 25th book for Temptation. This talented author lives with her family in Arkansas, where she's busy plotting out her next 25 books.

Books by Gina Wilkins

HARLEQUIN TEMPTATION

Gina Wilkins
A WISH FOR LOVE

Harlequin Books

TORONTO • NEW YORK • LONDON
AMSTERDAM • PARIS • SYDNEY • HAMBURG
STOCKHOLM • ATHENS • TOKYO • MILAN
MADRID • WARSAW • BUDAPEST • AUCKLAND

ISBN 0-373-25692-2

A WISH FOR LOVE

Copyright © 1996 by Gina Wilkins.

This edition published by arrangement with Harlequin Books S.A.

Printed in U.S.A.

Prologue

February 14, 1921

THE BULLET SLAMMED into his chest with the force of a locomotive. Ian staggered, trying desperately to regain his footing, only dimly aware of what had just happened to him.

The night was cloudy and cold, and had been peaceful until the gunshot shattered the silence. Ian Cameron and his twin sister, Mary Anna, had been walking, sharing a few moments of solitude in the winter-bare gardens while a noisy party raged inside the inn. They'd heard a sound from the old caretaker's shack, had seen a light they couldn't explain, and Ian had decided to investigate, despite Anna's misgivings.

They had just spotted three men coming out of the shack, when one of them, his face hidden in shadows, had fired a weapon.

Ian's only clear thought as he crumpled to the ground was deep regret that he hadn't listened to Anna's warnings. His stubbornness had finally gotten him into trouble, as others had been expecting for years. And he'd brought Anna down with him.

Anna, he thought as dark clouds seemed to descend from the skies to engulf him. *I'm so sorry. I've always tried to take care of you . . . and now I've failed.*

As though from very far away, he heard her scream. Heard the agony in her voice as she cried his name. "Ian! Oh, God, *no!*"

He wanted to speak, to comfort her, to tell her he loved her. He wasn't given the chance. The soft touch of her trembling fingers on his face was the last thing he knew.

October 31, 1960

ONE OF THE BOYS was covered head to toe in a ragged sheet with big, uneven holes cut for eyes. The other was a pint-size cowboy in an oversize felt hat, a fake-leather vest with the name Roy Rogers stamped across the back, neatly creased jeans, fancy-stitched boots and a cheap holster sporting two shiny toy guns.

The cowboy tugged down the red bandanna that had covered the lower half of his face and gave his sheeted friend a shove. "Go on," he urged. "I dare you. Unless you're chicken."

"I ain't chicken," the other boy protested. "But I don't want to get in trouble. My ma told me to stay away from this old inn. She says it's dangerous."

His companion squinted at the dark building looming ahead of them at the end of a tangled, overgrown pathway. "You're scared of the ghosts," he accused mockingly.

"Am not!" the spook in the sheet shouted. "My ma said there ain't no such thing as ghosts."

"Yeah? Well, how come you're scared to go touch the front door, huh? What are you, a sissy?"

"I ain't a sissy! You call me that again and I'll punch your lights out, Calvin Burton."

"Bobby's a sissy, Bobby's a sissy," Calvin sang out in a taunting rhythm.

Jerking the sheet off his head, the other boy, his face as red as his hair, doubled his fists and planted his feet belligerently. "You're so brave, *you* go touch the door," he dared. "And don't you ever call me a sissy again, or I'll tell Patty O'Neal that you wet the bed."

Calvin paled. "You better not tell her that, or I'll— I'll— " He couldn't think of any retribution horrible enough to equal Bobby's threat.

"So go touch the door."

Calvin gulped and glanced again at the inn, which suddenly looked so much larger. Darker. "I will if you will."

Bobby swallowed audibly. "O-okay. We'll go together."

The two brave heroes set their bulging bags of trick-or-treat candy on a big rock at the end of the walkway and squared their shoulders. And then, so close together they were almost touching, they moved slowly toward the deserted, reportedly haunted inn.

They'd gotten only halfway when they saw something move on the porch.

Two figures stood there looking at them. A dark-haired, scowling man in a strange dark suit. And a smiling, dark-haired woman in a long, floaty white dress.

The boys could see right through them.

For a long moment, they were paralyzed with fear, their mouths open as they stared at the apparitions. Bobby let out a shriek, which was swiftly echoed by his companion.

They turned on their heels and bolted down the path as though the devil, himself, were after them.

ANNA CLUCKED RUEFULLY. "Poor dears. We frightened them half silly. I didn't know they would see us."

Ian's scowl deepened. "Reduced to this," he muttered. "Terrifying adolescents on Halloween. How much longer are we supposed to go on this way, Anna?"

"I don't know," she murmured sympathetically, aware of how his restless nature rebelled against the shadowy, meaningless existence they'd been forced to endure since that deadly night in the garden. "But at least we're together. I can't bear to think what it would be like to be alone like this. Here—or at that other place. The gray place." She shuddered expressively.

Ian seemed to take some solace from her words. She had always been the only one who could truly soothe him.

"You're right, of course," he said, managing a faint smile for her. "I don't know what I would do without you. It was bad enough when Mother died. I only regret that I couldn't protect you from this. I still blame myself that your life ended with mine, when you had so much ahead of you."

"How many more times must we go through this?" she asked with a sigh. "This was meant to be, Ian. We were born together, and we died together. And now it appears that we'll spend eternity together."

"Frightening children," he grumbled.

She laughed softly. "At least we aren't forced to rattle chains."

He responded with a reluctant chuckle. "You find the best in everything, don't you, Anna?"

"I try."

His smile faded. "You don't deserve this. You should have had more."

She touched his face, and though neither of them could feel the contact, the gesture was comforting to both. "I have *you*, Ian. That's enough for me."

August 1, 1996

IT WAS A CLEAR, late-summer night in the garden. A billion stars glittered brightly overhead, and the scent of fresh-blooming flowers hung heavily in the air.

There were lights burning in the windows of the inn. Recently reopened for business, it wasn't quite full, but several of the rooms were occupied, and the increasingly popular dining room had just closed after a busy evening. Silhouetted against the curtains in one downstairs-bedroom window, two shadows merged in what might have been a passionate kiss.

At the end of the garden path, Ian stood looking at that window. His usually hard, firm mouth curved into a very faint smile. He still couldn't explain how Anna had been given a new life, an opportunity to love and to have the family she'd always wanted so badly, but he hadn't for one moment begrudged her good fortune.

Maybe he had earned his lonely fate through the rebellion of his youth, but Anna was different. She was special. She deserved another chance. And it had been miraculously granted her. Ian could take pleasure in that, if nothing else.

An owl hooted above him, undisturbed by his presence. The light went out in the bedroom, leaving its occupants in the quiet intimacy of darkness.

Ian nodded in satisfaction, turned and faded silently into the shadows.

Alone.

1

February 16, 1896

My babies are two days old, diary. My twins. Ian and Mary Anna. How surprised, and how delighted James would have been to see them both, so healthy and so very beautiful. Already they resemble him, with their dark hair and dark eyes. Just looking at them is almost like having him with me. Almost.

I will not cry. I've spent so much of the past three months in tears. At first, I wondered if it were possible to go on without James. I did not believe I would ever smile again. And then I saw our babies.

No more tears. I must think of the children now. And of the inn, their legacy from the father who loved them so much, though he did not live to see them.

They were his final gift to me—born on Valentine's Day. And though I know it sounds foolish, I made a special wish for them on the night they were born. I prayed that they would not leave this earth without finding the love my darling James and I were fortunate enough to share. I wished that they would each meet someone who would love them

absolutely, and that they would feel that same unconditional love in their own hearts. Would that I
had the power to grant my own request for them.

Despite the pain I have endured since losing
James, I pray my children will know a love like ours
in their lifetime. The joy I found with James, and
that I feel now when I gaze into the tiny faces of our
children, is well worth any price I have paid.

October 10, 1996

BAILEY GATES didn't intentionally eavesdrop on the private conversation between her brother and sister-in-law.
She had been sitting alone for the past hour in the gazebo Dean had recently built in the garden of his rural-
Arkansas inn.

The inn was over a hundred years old, impeccably restored and listed on the register of local historic places.
Dean had been faithful to the original designs in his renovations, making it easy for guests to believe they had
stepped back in time. Even the new additions were de-
signed to blend with the old styles. The gazebo, with its
charmingly curved lines and fussy gingerbread, was a
good example of Dean's eye for historic detail. The tiny
cottage where Bailey was staying was just finished, but
it, too, looked as though it had been here for years.

Dean intended the little cottage to be the first of several grouped around the main building, for honeymooners and other guests who wanted extra privacy.
When he and Anna had learned there was a baby on the

way, he'd changed his plans for this first cottage. He'd decided to designate it as staff housing and make it available to the housekeeper and her daughter, freeing their rooms in the inn for use as a nursery.

And then Bailey had shown up unexpectedly on his doorstep only a couple of days after the cottage was completed, and he had insisted that she stay as long as she liked, since they wouldn't be needing a nursery for several months.

She had accepted his offer gratefully—more gratefully than she'd allowed him to see, actually. She'd been here a week.

She desperately needed that private sanctuary just now.

It was a beautiful afternoon, bright and cloudless, warm enough for comfort in her light sweater and jeans. An open book lay in her lap, but she hadn't been reading. She'd been looking at the old inn and dreaming of days gone by, imagining what it must have been like a hundred years earlier, back when life was simpler, more refined.

An antiques dealer, Bailey knew she tended to romanticize the past, mentally glossing over the hardships her ancestors had faced in daily life. Still, it was a harmless enough pastime for her to daydream of social graces, elegant clothing and dashing, adventurous men of honor.

The sort of men she found sadly lacking in the modern world, no matter how long she'd waited to find one.

She shuddered as her thoughts turned briefly to the last man she'd become involved with. She was still appalled that she had misjudged him so badly. So dangerously.

He'd seemed so nice. She'd never guessed at the darker side of him. Not until he'd begun to stalk her.

Her brother's voice was a welcome distraction from that unpleasant reminder of her former gullibility. And her worry.

"Sweetheart, I thought you *wanted* to go on this vacation. We've discussed it for months," he was saying.

Automatically, Bailey turned toward the sound. A row of huge azalea bushes, still green and leafy even late in October, shielded her brother and his wife from sight. Bailey opened her mouth to let them know she was there, but Anna spoke before Bailey could say anything.

"Oh, Dean, you know I want to go away with you," Anna said, her musical voice soft with love for her husband of eight months. "It's just . . . hard for me to leave here. When I think about our departure tomorrow morning, my chest tightens so much I can hardly breathe."

Bailey frowned, surprised. Why was Anna so averse to leaving? Her sister-in-law had never seemed the least bit timid. Just the opposite, in fact.

"Anna, we need this time alone before the baby comes. It's our last chance for a real honeymoon. Aunt Mae and Cara are perfectly capable of running the inn for a few weeks, especially at this time of year, and now Bailey's here to help out if they need her. Do you really want to let this opportunity pass us by?"

Dean sounded so patient, so enticing. Bailey couldn't help smiling at the differences she'd noticed in her brother during the past year or so. Once he'd been an up-and-coming workaholic marketing executive in Chicago, intense, stressed, impatient, unhappily married. After his divorce from his first wife—an event Bailey still secretly celebrated—he'd deliberately made changes.

He'd walked away from the income and the prestige of his former career to buy this old inn in tiny Destiny, Arkansas. And he'd fallen head over heels in love for the first time in his life. He and Anna had married after a whirlwind courtship, the details of which Bailey had never quite figured out, and were blissfully expecting a baby in six months.

Bailey was delighted to observe that her brother looked genuinely happy now for the first time in years. He laughed, he relaxed, he enjoyed, but most noticeably he almost glowed with love for his lovely, dark-haired wife. Even if Bailey hadn't taken immediately to Anna—which she had—she would have loved her just for making Dean so happy. It was the type of happiness that had always eluded Bailey, to her regret.

"I'm being silly, I suppose," Anna murmured, her voice just audible to Bailey through the bushes that lay between them.

"I understand," Dean responded quietly. "You're thinking about your brother."

Bailey's eyebrows rose sharply. *Brother?* This was the first she'd heard of Anna's having a brother.

"Yes. I—I know he's been . . . gone for months, but I can't bear to think that he might still be just drifting, all alone. I suppose I'm afraid to leave because I cling to the hope that he'll come back to me someday. Somehow. What if I'm not here when he tries to reach me?"

Dean's sigh was as expressive, as sympathetic as his words. "I understand, darling. We'll cancel the trip, if it makes you feel better. We don't need a seaside resort for a honeymoon. We've been having a beautiful honeymoon right here."

"Oh, Dean, I really am being silly, aren't I? We can't spend all our time secluded here, waiting for something that will probably never happen. We have lives to lead, and . . . and he would want me to live mine to the fullest. We'll only be gone for a couple of weeks, and I intend to enjoy every day of it. I really want to be alone with you in a tropical paradise."

"That sounds wonderful," Dean said fervently. "But are you sure, Anna? Really sure? I only want you to be happy. I never want you to regret choosing to stay with me, even though it meant being separated from your brother."

"I have never regretted my decision for one moment," his wife replied, sounding more like the confident, decisive Anna that Bailey had come to know. "I'll see my brother again someday. And in the meantime, I'm very happy here with you. With our inn. And soon we'll have a child. I've told you many times, Dean, and it's still true—if I had it to do over, I would still choose you."

There was a rustle of movement, followed by an unintelligible murmur. The significance was unmistakable. And suddenly Bailey realized that she'd been blatantly eavesdropping on an intimate conversation.

Her cheeks flamed as though she'd actually been caught in the act. How embarrassing.

She quickly hid her face behind her book, pretending great interest in the historical romance unfolding within its pages. Maybe if he spotted her like this, he would think she was too absorbed in her reading to have paid attention to his conversation.

To Bailey's relief, Dean and Anna went back inside a few moments later, presumably without having realized that they'd had an audience. Her lip caught between her teeth, Bailey looked toward the inn, unable to stop thinking about what she'd overheard.

Why was Anna so reluctant to leave? It wasn't as if she'd spent her entire life here, though the Cameron Inn had been built by her great-great uncle. As far as Bailey knew, Anna had visited the inn for the first time less than a year ago, to research her family history. That was when she had somehow met and fallen in love with Dean, though no one in the family had even known Dean was dating anyone until he'd announced his engagement.

Why had Anna told everyone she had no living family? Why had she never mentioned her brother? Why had Dean made it sound as though Anna had been forced to choose between him and her brother? Had her brother so opposed the match that he'd severed all ties with her because of it? Surely not. Couldn't he see that Anna and Dean were perfect for each other?

Bailey only wished *she* could find someone who made her feel the way Dean obviously did when he looked at his beloved wife. After her last disastrous attempt at a relationship, she was beginning to believe it would never happen for her.

BAILEY WASN'T the only eavesdropper that afternoon. In one shadowy corner of the gazebo, Ian stood thoughtfully watching Bailey. He'd been there for some time.

Ian found her fascinating to watch. Her face seemed to mirror all her emotions, her expressions changing swiftly, revealingly.

She obviously appreciated the inn. She smiled when she looked at it, her blue eyes soft and dreamy. He liked that.

She frowned when her thoughts turned inward. Something was bothering her, making her unhappy. Occasionally, she scowled as though in self-castigation. Once or twice, she'd looked utterly disheartened.

He wondered who had hurt her. And why she seemed to blame herself.

He, too, overheard the conversation between Dean and Anna. He frowned when he heard the grief in Anna's voice as she explained why she was reluctant to leave the inn. He didn't want Anna to grieve. She had been given a chance to live, to love, to *be* loved. Ian was happy for her.

If only there was some way he could let her know. He'd tried, but to no avail. He simply couldn't reach her.

Though he was usually able to accept his lonely fate with resignation, if not equanimity, there were times when he thought the overwhelming frustration with his lack of control would drive him insane. Whatever mistakes he'd made in his twenty-five years of life, whatever sins he'd committed, there could have been no worse punishment than to take away his uncompromising command of his own destiny.

He was relieved when Anna finally agreed to go on the trip with her husband. He hoped she would enjoy it. Something told him Dean would make sure that she did. From what Ian had seen, there was little Dean Gates would deny his bride. To be perfectly honest, he was spoiling her. Ian smiled indulgently, thinking that no one deserved to be spoiled more than Anna.

The couple went into the inn and Ian turned his attention back to Bailey. She had buried her nose in her book. Her cheeks were pink from embarrassment. Because she'd overheard a private conversation? It wasn't as though she'd been sneaking around, trying to hear something not meant for her ears.

She really was a very attractive woman. Her hair was shorter than he might have liked, swinging in a soft bob just below her chin, but he liked the brown-shot-with-red color. Her eyes were blue, with long, dark lashes. Small nose, firm chin, sweetly curved mouth. She was of medium height and on the slender side. Her legs looked long and shapely in the dungarees she wore with an oversize green sweater. Hardly feminine garments, but she looked decidedly feminine in them.

He'd been watching her for almost a week now, since she'd arrived at the inn with the excuse to her family that she needed some time away from her work. A leave of absence, she'd called it. Nothing was wrong, she'd said too casually. She was just tired and needed a few weeks' vacation.

Her brother had looked skeptical, but hadn't pressed. Ian, too, had thought her excuses were patently flimsy, especially when combined with the forlorn look that occasionally crossed her face.

Bailey had made a valiant attempt at hiding her problems from the other residents of the inn. She'd smiled brightly at her aunt, Mae Harper, and at the housekeeper, Cara McAlister, and her young daughter, Casey. Her smiles faded only when she was alone—or when she thought she was alone.

She would have been startled to learn that she wasn't alone quite as often as she believed.

Now, for instance.

Ian watched as Bailey glanced up from her book, looked cautiously around, then closed the book and stood.

She stretched, and the movement pulled her thin sweater tight across her nicely full breasts. He felt the tug of attraction and smiled grimly, thinking what a useless response that was from someone in his state.

Bailey walked away, toward the inn, and Ian faded into the grayness, still wondering what it would take to put a smile into her melancholy blue eyes. And wondering what it was about her that made him wish he could try.

ALONG WITH BAILEY, the entire staff of the Cameron Inn gathered in the lobby the next morning to see the owner and his wife off on their belated honeymoon. Aunt Mae was the first to step forward for a farewell kiss. She had been with Dean at the inn from the beginning, helping him through renovations and the opening for business six months later, and now staying on as the inn's hostess.

Short and plump, her hair dyed a bright coppery red, sixty-something Mae Harper looked like everyone's idea of a favorite aunt—except for her rather eccentric taste in clothing and accessories. This morning, she wore a black sweater appliquéd with huge satin flowers and studded with multicolored stones, red stretch pants, half a dozen jangling bracelets and dangling red-and-black earrings. Her eyeglasses were also red, and accented with rhinestones. Beneath the color and glitter lay the warmest heart and purest soul Bailey had ever encountered.

"Now don't you waste one minute of your vacation worrying about this place, you hear?" Mae demanded as she tugged her nephew's head down for a smacking kiss that left a smear of crimson on his cheek. "We are perfectly capable of running the place without your supervision for a few weeks."

"You have the telephone number of the resort?" Dean asked.

"I have the number of the resort," she answered patiently. "And the number for the plumber. And the electrician. And anyone else I could possibly need during the next three weeks."

Dean chuckled. "Sorry, Aunt Mae. Old habits die hard."

Mae smiled and moved on to speak to Anna.

Still waiting her turn, Bailey watched as Cara and Casey McAlister stepped forward. Bailey was intrigued by the beautiful housekeeper and her shy, sweet daughter. Dean had told Bailey that the pair had arrived at the inn when renovations were barely under way, long before he was ready to hire staff. He had found himself unable to turn them away.

He'd told Bailey that he had never regretted his decision; Cara had proven to be a loyal and hardworking employee who fully earned her pay. Little Casey had caused no problems—just the opposite, in fact. Everyone doted on her.

Dean still knew very little about what he suspected was an unhappy history for the two, which had left them quiet and wary and slow to form outside bonds, but he said that everyone had noticed that they seemed happier and more secure with each passing week.

The cook, Elva Tippin, and the two other members of the kitchen staff all reiterated that the Cameron Inn and its dining room were in excellent hands for the next three weeks. Millie, the part-time maid, waved a quick salute as she hurried upstairs to make beds and vacuum. And then everyone went back to work, leaving Bailey alone in the beautifully decorated lobby with her brother and sister-in-law.

Dean took Bailey's hands in his, looking searchingly into her face. "Will you still be here when we get back?"

He'd asked before, but she hadn't been able to give him a firm answer. She was no closer to doing so now. As long as her past didn't catch up with her . . . "Probably," she hedged. "I really have no definite plans right now. Of course, if you need the cottage, I'll . . ."

"Don't be ridiculous," Dean interrupted brusquely. "The cottage is yours for as long as you want it. Got that?"

She smiled and kissed the part of his cheek that wasn't marked by their aunt's lipstick. "Thanks, Dean."

He hugged her. "You'll be okay?" His gruff tone, and the concern behind it, let her know that he'd never really accepted the vague excuses she'd given when she'd arrived unexpectedly a week ago.

She'd told him that she'd simply been tired and in need of a break from work and routine. That she'd made the decision impulsively, almost whimsically. That he wasn't to worry about her, she was fine. She'd lied, of course. She'd just hoped he wouldn't realize it quite so quickly. She should have known better. Her older brother had always understood her better than anyone else in the world.

Anna moved closer, a smile in her dark eyes. "Stay as long as you like," she told Bailey. "In fact, I wish you would stay on permanently. It's so nice having family all together."

There was a hint of a catch in her voice. Bailey now understood that Anna was thinking of her own brother—whatever the circumstances of their separation.

Dean pulled his bride away a moment later. "We'd better go," he said gently. "We have a plane to catch."

Anna shivered. "I still can't believe I agreed to actually get on one of those things."

Bailey was puzzled. Anna made it sound as though she'd never flown before. How had she gotten from London, where she said she'd been raised, to central Arkansas? Bailey still thought it odd that Anna's only faintly British accent was notably stronger at some times more than others.

There seemed to be a lot of unanswered questions about Bailey's charming sister-in-law.

Anna and Dean paused in the doorway. Anna looked around the lobby, her expression so torn that Bailey's heart twisted in sympathy, even though she didn't understand what was behind her sister-in-law's distress.

"We'll be back soon," Anna said, apparently speaking to the inn, itself. "I'll miss you every day."

She turned abruptly, her voice thickening. "Let's go," she said to Dean.

Dean wrapped an arm around his wife's shoulders and led her outside, leaving Bailey staring thoughtfully at the door they closed behind them.

She thought of the love she'd sensed between them, the almost palpable bond connecting them. And her heart twinged with longing. Again, she wished she could find someone with whom she could share that special closeness.

With little hope, she wished . . .

IN A FAR CORNER of the lobby, Ian stood with his hands in his pockets, his attention also focused on the front door. "Have a wonderful time, Anna," he murmured, unheard. "I'll miss you, too."

He glanced at Bailey, who still stood in the center of the lobby, looking so sad and wistful. So alone.

He understood loneliness, all too well. And now, he was painfully aware of the uselessness and meaninglessness of his present existence.

If only there was something worthwhile he could do. Anything that would relieve the boredom. The grayness. The soul-numbing solitude.

Though he hadn't been known as a particularly empathetic or sensitive man during his lifetime, Ian suddenly wished he could somehow ease this woman's obvious pain. Make her smile. Preferably at him.

He desperately needed something to make him remember how it had felt to be alive.

Seething with frustration and futility, he wished . . .

ON THE THIRD AFTERNOON after Dean and Anna's departure, Bailey went out to the gazebo with her book, as had become her habit after lunch. It wasn't that she didn't enjoy being inside the beautifully restored old inn with its comfortable antique and reproduction furnishings, many of which she'd located for her brother through the shop she'd worked for in Chicago. And she'd certainly been made welcome by everyone. It was just that she still felt like an outsider, particularly at this time of day, when everyone was busy with chores and routine responsibilities.

The few other guests were off sightseeing or shopping. The kitchen staff was cleaning up after lunch and preparing for the evening meal, when the dining room would again open for local business. Cara and the part-time maid were cleaning, Aunt Mae was busy with paperwork, little Casey was in school. Everyone seemed to have something productive to do. Everyone but Bailey.

She'd offered to help—cleaning, cooking, bookkeeping. She'd been politely refused. She wasn't really needed, she thought. Here—or anywhere. But she was getting maudlin. Again.

Just because her career had fallen to pieces and her latest romance had seemed more like the movie *Fatal Attraction,* there was no reason to sit around moping, feeling sorry for herself. She had more spirit than that. Or at least, she'd always believed she did.

With her book unopened in her lap, she leaned her head wearily against the back of the built-in bench and wondered if she would ever get her life back together.

When she opened her eyes again, there was a man standing in one corner of the gazebo, watching her.

Catching her breath in surprise, she cocked her head to study him. She didn't remember seeing him around the inn before—and if she'd seen him, she certainly would have remembered. The man was extraordinary. Dark hair, worn a bit long on top and in the back, with neat sideburns. Glittering dark eyes, framed with black lashes. Strong face, lean build. Age—somewhere between twenty-five and thirty, she'd guess. Gorgeous.

He could have stepped straight from her fantasies.

"Hello," she said, feeling ridiculously shy as she tried to conceal her startled reaction to him. "Where did you come from?"

2

February 14, 1898

Today is the children's second birthday. Quite an occasion, with all the staff helping us celebrate. Cook made Ian's favorite dish—baked chicken with rice—and a chocolate cake for dessert. The children were covered with chocolate when they'd finished!

Two years old. They grow so quickly. They are good children, though spirited. Ian will be a heartbreaker someday, with his large dark eyes and his rare, mischievous smiles. So like his father. He is very affectionate with me, a bit serious in nature and already quite protective of his sister. We shall have to watch that temper of his, though.

Mary Anna is the impulsive one. She dashes in without fear of consequence. I hope she will outgrow that reckless trait. So stubborn. So sweet. We all adore her—and she knows it, the little imp.

They seem happy, and secure. Though the inn keeps me busy, I spend as much time with them as I can, and the staff is good to help me with them. Still, it isn't easy raising them on my own, with all the responsibilities of the inn in addition to their needs. If only James—

I mustn't think that way. I have the children's future to consider, and dreaming of the past is no help to them. I have had several gentleman callers during the past months. Mr. Carpenter, the owner of the Destiny Diner, is among the more persistent. I do not attribute my popularity to my personal charms, whatever they might be. I'm afraid the inn is my most seductive asset. Mr. Carpenter makes little secret of his interest in the business. He tells me that I shouldn't be bothering myself with the details of running an inn, that under his guidance, the establishment could become quite successful. He must think I am not at all bright. The Cameron Inn is quite successful now, without benefit of his assistance. My James taught me well.

Oh, James. It is difficult to consider giving even a small part of myself to another man. But I am only twenty-five. And our children need a father.

If only you could have stayed with us.

CAUGHT OFF GUARD by Bailey's friendly greeting, Ian blinked, then looked over his shoulder. No one stood behind him. She was looking directly at him. Could it be?

"Were you talking to me?" he asked warily, almost certain she wouldn't be able to hear him.

Her soft mouth curved into a smile. "Of course. You're the only one here, aren't you?"

She could see him.

Ian sagged against the gazebo post behind him. He didn't feel it, but he needed the symbolic support. "I, er—"

"I haven't seen you at the inn before. You must have just arrived."

He nodded, wondering what, exactly, he should say. Wondering what the hell was going on.

She chuckled. "You really startled me. I closed my eyes for a moment, and when I opened them, there you were. Almost as if you appeared out of thin air."

His answering smile felt strained. "Not likely."

Her too-perceptive blue eyes searched his face. He wondered exactly what she saw. Could she tell that he was . . . different? When her eyes suddenly narrowed, he tensed, prepared to try to explain what defied explanation.

"Have we met before?" she asked unexpectedly.

"No. We haven't met."

"Oh. My mistake. It's just that there's something about you that seems so familiar, and yet—not exactly. Something about your eyes and your . . . Oh, I'm sorry. I'm babbling. I do that sometimes," she said a bit ruefully.

He remembered wishing that she would smile at him. She was doing so now, and he was standing there like a tongue-tied idiot.

He didn't understand why she could suddenly see him when she couldn't before. Or what he should do or say now that she could.

"Have you checked in yet?" she asked.

"Checked in? Er, no."

"I know there are rooms available for tonight," she said, obviously trying to make conversation. "It's a lovely hotel. My brother is the owner," she added with a faint touch of pride.

"Is he?" He tried to remember how to make small talk. It had been so damn long since he'd needed to. "It looks very nice. Old."

"It was built in the mid-1800s. Dean, my brother, re-cently restored it. He and his wife are away for a short vacation now, but the inn is fully staffed and very effi-ciently managed."

His smile deepened. "You make it sound very invit-ing."

"Did I sound like an advertisement? Sorry." An at-tractive pink hue rose in her cheeks. Then, she said, "Oh, we haven't even introduced ourselves, have we? I'm Bai-ley Gates." She looked at him expectantly.

I'm Ian Cameron. And by the way, I've been dead for over seventy-five years.

He couldn't tell her that, of course. Obviously—and quite surprisingly—she saw nothing about him to make her think he was any different from the men of her time. He found himself unwilling to turn her friendly smile into a look of shock or disbelief. Or worse, fear.

"Call me Bran," he said.

"Bran?" she repeated as though she wasn't sure she'd heard him correctly.

He nodded. The name had popped into his head out of his distant memories. Now that he thought about it, he recognized the irony of his choice. "Bran. It's an old Celtic name. My mother liked it."

His mother had read him the legend of Prince Bran of Ireland countless times during his childhood. The nightly stories had stopped when she'd married his stepfather. Ian could no longer remember whether stopping the pleasurable pastime had been his mother's choice, or his own.

He grimly suspected that it had been his own sullen rebellion that had put an end to the formerly treasured bedtime ritual.

"And your last name?" Bailey asked.

"Bran will do."

She frowned. "A mystery man, are you?" she asked, looking disgruntled.

He chuckled. She reminded him just then of her idiosyncratic and plainspoken aunt, whom he'd watched and enjoyed on occasion during the past year.

"A very private man," he replied, wondering if she would take offense.

If she did, she didn't allow it to show. "Whatever. If you like, I'll take you to the front desk so you can check in. The dining room opens for dinner at five, and—"

"Thank you, but I won't need a room," Ian cut in. "I have a place. I was just looking around the inn out of curiosity," he added, sensing the need for some explanation of his presence.

"But—"

He felt the slight tugging sensation that signaled the end of his time here. When he would return—if ever—

was up to the whims of whatever force controlled his fate.

He took a step toward the gazebo's opening. "I must go now."

"So soon?" She stood, looking oddly disappointed. Or was that only wishful thinking on his part?

"Will you be in the area long?" she asked. "I'd be happy to give you a tour of the inn sometime, if you're interested in historic buildings. It has quite a colorful past."

He managed not to wince. "I'm sure it does. I'd, er, like to hear about it, but I'm not sure I'll be able to return."

"Oh. Well, it was very nice to meet you, Bran."

He stepped onto the rock path that wound through the gardens, and then turned, feeling the need to say something more. He'd been given the opportunity to meet her, talk to her, have her smile at him, even if only this once. Even if he could see that her smiles didn't extend to her lovely eyes.

Something was still hurting her . . . and worrying her. Something she couldn't share with the family she obviously cared for very deeply. Maybe there was a reason that she'd seen him, heard him. Maybe he was supposed to help her.

For some reason, he wanted very much to help Bailey Gates, though there was nothing he could do to help himself.

Life was too short, too precious a gift to spend it being unhappy—or angry. He had learned that lesson the hard way. Maybe there was something he could say to make it easier for Bailey to reach that valuable conclusion.

He would like to think he had accomplished something worthwhile—no matter how small—during the all-too-brief time he'd had with her.

"Bailey?" The feel of her name on his tongue was strangely intriguing.

She looked at him in question. "Yes?"

He shoved his hands into the pockets of his dark slacks. "You have a lovely smile. Don't forget how to use it."

He hurried away then, quickly putting bushes and trees between them so that she wouldn't know exactly where he'd gone. As he felt the grayness overtake him, he grimaced at the inanity of his parting words to her. Unfortunately, he'd never been skilled with flowery, morally uplifting phrases. He'd always left that sort of thing to Anna.

He'd never regretted his lack of talent in that area—until now.

"BAILEY? Are you listening to me?"

Bailey blinked and made herself focus on her aunt, who sat in a nearby chair in the inn's small, private sitting room. They'd finished dinner a half hour earlier and had retired to the sitting room to visit before Bailey went back to the cottage for the night.

Her needlework in her lap, Mae was watching Bailey with a concerned frown. Bailey hadn't realized how long she'd been sitting in silence, thinking of the man she'd met that afternoon.

"I'm sorry, Aunt Mae. My attention wandered. I didn't mean to be rude. What were you saying?"

"I asked if you've enjoyed your stay here so far."

"Oh, yes, of course. Very much. The inn is just beautiful and the meals have been delicious. It's no wonder the dining room is becoming so popular with the locals."

"You haven't gotten out at all since you arrived. Wouldn't you like to see the area? Do some shopping or sightseeing?"

"I've been resting. I needed to be lazy for a few days."

"You did look exhausted when you arrived. Quentin's been working you too hard at that shop, hasn't he?"

Bailey smiled ruefully. "You know Quentin," she prevaricated.

Mae huffed. "Yes, I know Quentin. He's a petty, unreasonable, self-absorbed, egotistical, tyrannical—"

Bailey laughed, despite herself. "All right, that's enough. I know you never liked him. For that matter, everyone knows it. Including Quentin."

Like her aunt, Bailey had never been one to hide her opinions behind a mask of polite fabrication. It was a trait that had finally gotten her fired, though she hadn't yet mentioned it to her family.

"I don't know how on earth you managed to convince him to give you a leave of absence," Mae went on. "He always acted as though he couldn't do without you for a weekend, much less for—how many weeks did you say you're taking off?"

"I haven't really decided yet," Bailey hedged. She didn't want to lie to her aunt, but she wasn't ready to let everyone know what a mess her life was in right now. It was too humiliating.

Mae peered at her niece through her red-framed glasses, her softly lined face pensive. "Would you like to talk about it, dear? You know I'm always ready to listen when you have a problem. Perhaps it would help to share it."

Bailey blinked back a quick rush of tears, refusing to give in to them. She hadn't cried in years; she wouldn't start now. Not over Quentin. And certainly not over Larry, the man she'd invested so much time and effort into recently, only to find herself fearing for her safety because of him.

She sighed. "Thanks, Aunt Mae, but I'm not ready to talk about it just yet, okay?"

"Whenever you're ready, I'll be here."

"I know. And it means the world to me."

She quickly changed the subject. "Mark Winter seems very nice. I enjoyed visiting with him during dinner. I can see why he and Dean have become such good friends."

Mark was the editor of the local newspaper, the *Destiny Daily*, and a frequent visitor at the inn. When he'd shown up for dinner at the same time Mae and Bailey were being seated, Mae had invited him to join them, an invitation he'd accepted with obvious pleasure. He seemed fond of Mae, and had treated her with respect, which had inclined Bailey to like him at once.

"Mark is a fine young man," Mae said with a smile. "We see him often. He says he likes the food we serve much better than his own bachelor fare."

"I don't think it's the food that keeps him coming here."

Mae sighed softly. "You noticed that, did you?"

"How could I have helped it? Every time Cara entered the room, Mark all but fell into his plate. He's obviously crazy about her."

"Yes. I believe he fell in love with her the first time he saw her, only a few days after she came to work for us nine months ago. He's asked her out at least twice a week since."

"And how many times has she accepted?"

Mae sighed more deeply. "None."

"She isn't interested in him?"

"To be honest, it's hard to tell. Cara keeps so much to herself. There are times when I've seen her looking at him, and I thought . . . well, anyway, she's done everything she can to discourage his attentions. But she's learning, as the rest of us have, that Mark is a persistent man. He's very polite about it. He asks her nicely if she'd like to go out, she firmly turns him down, and he smiles and says maybe some other time. They've played that scene so many times, it's become almost a habit whenever their paths cross."

Bailey pictured Mark's warm and deceptively lazy smile. "I can't imagine why Cara won't give him a chance. He seems like such a nice guy," she commented.

"Dean thinks Cara had a disastrous relationship in her past, possibly an abusive husband. He thinks she's been burned so badly that she's afraid to try again."

Bailey winced. "Yeah, I guess that makes sense." Actually, it was all too easy for her to understand, especially after her own latest fiasco. Getting involved with an abusive male tended to wreak havoc with a woman's self-confidence. And her peace of mind.

"You seemed quite taken with Mark, yourself. Could it be that you're considering giving Cara some competition?"

Bailey shook her head firmly. "Oh, no. As much as I like him, I'm not interested in chasing a man who is so obviously in love with another woman. Give me credit for more sense than that, Aunt Mae."

Had she been perfectly honest, she would have added that there had been no real spark of attraction between her and Mark. She hadn't caught her breath when he'd smiled, or found herself trapped in his gaze, or oddly, disconcertingly drawn to him.

The only man who'd affected her in that manner lately had been a dark-haired, dark-eyed stranger who hadn't even given her his last name.

For at least the hundredth time that evening, she replayed that strange conversation in the gazebo. She wondered where he had come from, where he'd gone when he left her. Why he'd seemed so reluctant to divulge anything about himself.

For all she knew, he could be a criminal. Or a certified nut case like Larry.

And yet something about him had made her trust him from the first moment she'd seen him standing there. Which only went to show that she hadn't learned any lasting lessons from Larry, after all, she thought in self-disgust.

In contrast to Mark Winter's sandy-haired boy-next-door looks and laughing green eyes, the man who'd called himself Bran had been dark and brooding, his black eyes revealing little emotion. Mark was on the loose-limbed, lanky side; Bran's slender, lethal grace-fulness had made her think of a black jungle cat. A dangerous one.

Lifting her chin in defiance of her own trouble-prone nature, Bailey told herself that the two men had only one thing in common. She had no intention of getting personally involved with either one of them.

HAVING AWAKENED EARLY after a restless night, Bailey happened to be outside on Friday when a bright yellow school bus stopped to pick up Casey for school. She watched as Cara kissed her daughter's cheek and hugged her tightly for a moment before releasing her.

Cara watched as the bus drove out of sight before she turned back toward the inn. Only then did she see Bailey. "Oh. Good morning."

Bailey smiled. "It is a beautiful morning, isn't it? Fall is my favorite time of year."

It was going to be a glorious day. The air was crisp and fragrant. The huge old trees surrounding the inn had not yet dropped their brightly colored autumn leaves, red and orange and yellow against the backdrop of cloudless blue sky. For the first time in months, Bailey felt relaxed. Almost happy.

"It is a nice day," Cara agreed, pushing her honeyblond hair away from her fair-skinned oval face. "Do you have plans?"

"Dean left me the keys to his car. I thought I might drive into Hot Springs and do some sightseeing. Maybe check out the bathhouses. Hey, why don't you come with me?"

Cara's eyes widened in surprise. "Me? Oh, but I—"

"You can take a few hours off, can't you? It would be fun. You can show me around."

"I haven't spent much time in Hot Springs," Cara admitted. "I've only been there once or twice to take Casey to the dentist."

"Then we can both play tourist. What do you say?"

Cara twisted her slender hands in front of her. "I really should be here when Casey gets home. She—she worries when I'm not where she expects me to be."

Bailey wondered about that, but she merely smiled and nodded. "We'll be home before Casey. It's only a twenty-minute drive, isn't it?"

"Yes," Cara admitted slowly.

Bailey thought the other woman looked tempted but nervous. Why? Because she worried about taking a day off work? Or was there some other reason she was so reluctant to leave the safety of the inn?

"Look, I don't want to be pushy," Bailey said. "If you'd rather not go, or have things you need to do here, I understand."

Cara seemed to come to a sudden decision. "Actually, I think I would like to go," she said with a touch of shyness. "It sounds like fun. I haven't been out much lately."

"Great. I'll go tell Aunt Mae where we'll be."

"I have a few things to do very quickly," Cara said. "Can we leave in half an hour?"

"Sure. That'll give us plenty of time. Meet you in the lobby, okay?"

Cara smiled. "Okay."

Bailey was quite proud of herself. She'd decided that Cara McAlister needed to loosen up and enjoy herself more. That she needed a friend to encourage her to do so.

Bailey intended to become that friend.

She looked forward to getting away from the inn for a few hours. As much as she'd needed the break, she was becoming just a bit restless with nothing to occupy her time, especially when she was so accustomed to frantic activity and a never-ending list of demands on her time. And, to be frank, Cara wasn't the only one in need of a friend. Bailey could use one, herself.

She'd spent most of the night alternating between her regrets about her past, her worry about her future and her intense curiosity about the mysterious Bran, whom she hadn't seen since that odd interlude in the gazebo three days ago. She didn't want to spend all day watching for him, wondering if he would show up again. Foolishly hoping that he would. She needed to get out. And so did Cara, she reminded herself firmly.

Dean had often accused her of trying to solve everyone's problems except her own. She was too soft-hearted, he'd said. And much too confident in her own abilities. She thought there was nothing she couldn't fix, given time and patience. She even had an irksome habit of dating men with emotional baggage, men who needed her.

Dean had warned her that someday she was going to find that she'd taken care of everyone's needs except her own. She was going to feel used and unfulfilled, he'd predicted ominously.

Darned if he hadn't been right. She'd felt used and unfulfilled, all right. Thank God she'd taken to her heels before Larry had gotten a chance to hurt more than her pride and ego.

And yet here she was, making plans to stick her nose into poor Cara's life. She should know better, but—

Dean and Mae had known Cara had problems for almost a year now, and neither of them seemed to have made any attempt to try to help. Oh, sure, they'd probably say it was none of their business, but *someone* should make an effort, right? And if it wasn't going to be them, she supposed the responsibility had fallen to her.

She only hoped to heaven that this little project wouldn't turn out as badly as her last effort.

FROM THE SHADOWS of an oak tree at the edge of the inn's grounds, a man sipped coffee from an insulated container and grimaced at the bitter, lukewarm taste.

He'd been watching the place since dawn. He'd seen the kitchen staff arrive, and a small stream of locals pull in for breakfast in the public dining room. He'd watched the kid get on the school bus, and now his attention focused on the two women talking on the veranda. One of them, in particular.

His large fist tightened on the thin plastic cup. The sight of her smile made his eyes narrow in rage. She thought she was so clever. Thought she'd gotten away from him. Thought she was safe.

She thought wrong.

He was a patient man. He would choose his time carefully.

But he would have his revenge.

And there was nothing she—or any living person— could do to stop him.

3

March 10, 1899

Mary Anna almost burned down the inn today.

Poor dear, she didn't mean to cause such trouble. She was playing with a stick she'd poked into the fire while Emma was occupied with Ian. Before anyone knew it, the draperies in the sitting room were in flames. It is terrifying to think of the tragedy that could have resulted had not Emma acted so promptly and so efficiently. As it is, the damage will be expensive to repair.

With each day, it becomes more difficult for me to manage all the details of the inn as well as take care of the children. They are well-behaved, for the most part, but typically curious three-year-olds. They run us all ragged just keeping up with them.

My friends at church are still trying to convince me that I should give more consideration to marrying. They name several gentlemen who would be interested, though they must be aware that the inn is what really draws those men. I suppose it is clear to them that the inn is all that I truly have to offer; my love died with James. I cannot pretend otherwise.

Am I wrong to try to go on alone? Am I being selfish, insensitive to my children's needs? The thought of being another man's wife still distresses me, but I am considering the option. It is possible that it would be best for everyone.

Everyone, perhaps, but me.

IT WAS LATE, but Bailey couldn't sleep, even after an active day of shopping and sightseeing with Cara. Dressed for bed in a baggy pink T-shirt and matching knit shorts, she sat with her bare feet crossed beneath her on the bed in the little cottage, her chin propped in her hands as she replayed the day.

She liked Cara, though the other woman had been frustratingly reticent about herself. Bailey had come away with the impression that Cara was kindhearted, inclined to be a bit serious, somewhat shy and utterly devoted to her child.

Cara claimed to be widowed; her husband had died in a job-related accident when Casey was only a toddler. She'd said she had never been close to her husband's family, and that she had none of her own except a few distant cousins she'd never known well. She'd shared those tidbits only when Bailey had persistently asked questions under the guise of making conversation, but she hadn't elaborated, and had quickly changed the subject each time to something less personal.

The only thing Bailey had learned for certain was that Cara lived in fear, though she had no idea what frightened the other woman so. But something did. Cara was running—and had been for some time. Though she'd found a measure of security at the inn, and had obviously grown close to the friends she'd made here, it was obvious she was keeping a slight emotional distance from all of them.

Bailey would have bet that Cara was fully prepared to leave again at a moment's notice, and didn't want to form any ties that would bind her here.

Bailey found it extremely frustrating that she didn't know what Cara was so afraid of, and as a result had no idea how to help her. She might as well face it, she thought glumly. She was an incurable meddler.

Ms. Lonely Hearts was on the prowl again, ready to solve everyone's problems but her own. Maybe she was destined to spend the rest of her life this way, she thought with a dispirited sigh—taking care of everyone but herself.

And she was getting maudlin again, damn it.

Tossing her head back in defiance of her own depressing thoughts, she suddenly stood and crossed the sparsely furnished bedroom. Since the cottage had been completed only a few days before Bailey moved in, there had been little time for decorating. Dean had scrounged up a bed, a nightstand and chest for this room, as well as a love seat and two armchairs for the sitting room. The tiny kitchenette was still unfurnished. Bailey hadn't planned on doing any cooking while she was here, anyway.

A large cardboard box sat in one corner of the bedroom, the musty smell emanating from it competing with the lingering scent of fresh paint and newly finished woodwork. Aunt Mae had found the box of old books in the attic of the inn, and had asked Bailey to use her experience with antiques to determine if there was anything of value among the contents.

Though Bailey was certainly no expert on old books, she'd told her aunt that she didn't mind glancing through them. Maybe she'd find something worth having appraised, at least. And it would give her something meaningful to do, if only for a short time.

The first selections she glanced at were not particularly interesting. They were in poor shape, and wouldn't have been valuable had they been like new. She set them aside.

A little brown-covered book caught her attention. She lifted it out of the box, wrinkling her nose at the musty smell. It was a collection of bedtime stories, she noted, published just after the turn of the century.

The words were barely legible, and the once-colorful illustrations had faded, but something about the volume made Bailey smile. It looked as though it had been well-used, read and reread, treasured, perhaps, as a nighttime ritual between mother and child.

Whimsically, she pictured a slender woman in a Gibson-girl hairstyle and a long dress nestled on a bed beside her curly-haired child, reading by the soft light of an oil lamp. Her heart ached at the image. Bailey would love to have a child of her own to read to at night. Would she, like her fortunate sister-in-law, ever have that precious experience ahead of her?

Slowly, carefully, she leafed through the yellowed, badly foxed pages, stopping to read a line or two when she could make it out, wondering who might have bought the volume. According to the history her brother had researched so carefully, the inn would have still belonged to the original owners at the turn of the century. It had been built by a British immigrant named James Cameron, who'd died in an accident a few months before his young bride gave birth to tragedy-fated twins.

Her fingers stilled on the book's ragged cloth cover. Was it possible that this book had belonged to the legendary Cameron twins? she wondered, holding her breath as she considered the possibility. She added another tot to the mental image of mother and child.

She'd been enthralled by the history of the twins ever since she'd first heard about them, shortly after Dean had bought the inn. Some of the locals had claimed that their spirits haunted the old place. Dean had been interested in the legend, too, though he claimed that he'd looked into it only to debunk the ghost stories that had the potential to adversely affect his business.

He and Mark Winter had researched the much-embellished story, and had unwittingly uncovered a mystery that had gone unsolved for three-quarters of a century. Almost by accident, they had publicly unmasked a murderer long after the fact, to the avid fascination of the locals and the intense embarrassment of the murderer's prestigious descendants.

Ian and Mary Anna Cameron had been shot in cold blood by their stepbrother, Charles Peavy. Peavy and

Stanley Tagert, a crooked police officer in league with him, had spread the story that the twins had been involved in a profitable bootlegging operation. The twins were also blamed for the murder of a Prohibition officer. Peavy and Tagert had reported that the twins died in a shoot-out with Tagert when he'd tried to arrest them for their crimes.

Few had questioned the official story. None of the townspeople had ever realized that it was Charles who had headed the bootlegging ring; Charles who'd killed the Prohibition officer. Charles murdered the twins when they stumbled onto the truth about him. Using them as his cover, he had retired from his criminal activities after that point, going on to become a successful and respected businessman.

For seventy-five years, local history had recorded that Ian Cameron had died a criminal, and that his sister had either been his accomplice or had unfortunately died in the crossfire during the arrest attempt. Some people said that their ghosts haunted the old inn, a story that grew increasingly popular as the place suffered bankruptcy and decay during a long spell of mismanagement and neglect.

Dean and Mark had learned the truth when they'd located a witness to the murders, a dying man who'd been a frightened ten-year-old boy when Ian and Mary Anna were gunned down in front of him. Only a few weeks before his own death, the old man had told the whole story to Dean and Mark, and had provided proof of his claims. Mark had printed the sordid tale in his newspaper.

Bailey had suspected that there were specifics to the investigation that her brother hadn't shared with anyone, but no matter how many questions she'd asked, he hadn't given her any more details than Mark had published. Even now, Dean didn't like talking about the murders, or the ghost stories that had circulated around Valentine's Day each year—the date of the twins' birth and their death. Dean had never had much interest in the supernatural, and had little patience with what he'd called "crystal-carrying ghost groupies."

Bailey, on the other hand, loved a good legend—probably because of her fascination with the past.

She knew that some of the townspeople believed the spirits of the murdered twins had been freed when their murders had been solved and their names cleared. Others had seen no reason to embarrass a long-prominent family by publicizing something that had happened seventy-five years ago. Still others had savored the gossip and belated scandal.

It might have been her fanciful thoughts of ghosts and murders that made Bailey shiver. For the first time in over a week, she was aware of being alone in the little cottage.

It was silly, of course. The cottage was securely locked, well-lit on the outside and only a few yards from the inn. Telephones had been installed in the sitting room and bedroom, connecting directly to the front desk.

There was no reason at all for Bailey to be suddenly nervous.

She moistened her dry lips and told herself to stop being such a wimp. She'd been living alone for several years in Chicago and she didn't usually indulge in fearful imaginings.

She set the little brown book back on her nightstand and headed for the doorway. The dusty books had made her thirsty. She could use a glass of cold water.

She opened the bedroom door, stepped through it, then stopped with a muffled shriek when a tall, dark figure suddenly loomed in front of her. She was just about to make a screaming dash for safety when she recognized the intruder.

"Bran?" she asked hoarsely. "What are you doing here? How did you get in?"

He blinked, looking almost as startled by her entry as she had been at finding him there. He recovered immediately, his dark face taking on that carefully reserved expression she remembered so well, despite the very brief time she'd spent with him. "I'm sorry if I frightened you."

"You scared the hell out of me," she replied bluntly. "You're lucky I didn't call the cops."

"You probably should have," he commented. "*You're* lucky I'm not the dangerous type."

She eyed him uncertainly, thinking of the open bedroom door behind her and wondering how long it would take her to make it to the lock on the other side. "How do I know that you aren't dangerous?" she asked.

"I suppose you can't know for certain," he conceded. "You have only my word that I have no intention of harming you."

She felt a smile tug at the corners of her mouth. "Oh, that makes me feel so much better. I suppose a true criminal would tell me right away that he had nefarious purposes."

"An honest one would," Bran agreed solemnly.

She laughed. And then abruptly sobered when she realized that he still hadn't answered her questions. "What *are* you doing here?" she asked again.

"I, er, wanted to talk to you. About Anna," he added.

If he'd hoped to distract her from her doubts about his reasons for being in her cottage, he succeeded.

"Anna?" she asked, staring at him in surprise. "My sister-in-law?"

He nodded. "She and I grew up together. I understand she's away on vacation, but I was hoping you could tell me if she's well. And happy."

Bailey suddenly realized exactly what it was about Bran that had seemed so familiar to her when she'd first met him. He looked like Anna. So much so that he could easily be . . .

"You're her brother, aren't you?" she blurted out, covering her cheeks with her hands. "I should have realized it before. The resemblance between you and Anna is uncanny."

"You think so?" he murmured.

"Anna mentioned she had a brother," Bailey commented, seeing no need to add that she'd been eavesdropping at the time. "I got the impression that the two of you are estranged, and that she's very unhappy about it. She was hoping you would try to contact her soon. You *are* her brother, aren't you?"

He ran his thumb along the line of his jaw. She wondered why he always seemed to weigh his words so carefully, even in response to the simplest question.

Finally, he nodded. "I'm her brother."

Bailey immediately got defensive, remembering the rest of the overheard conversation between Anna and Dean. "What have you got against my brother? Dean is a wonderful, loving, kindhearted man. Your sister is lucky to be married to him!"

"I'm sure she is."

Bailey frowned. "You mean, you didn't oppose their marriage?"

"On the contrary. I urged my sister to do whatever would make her happy."

"Then why did Dean say that Anna was forced to choose between him and you?"

"Perhaps he simply meant that her loyalties naturally shifted to her husband when she married."

Bailey eyed him skeptically. "I don't think so."

"Then I really don't know."

"Maybe I'll ask him when he calls to check in. I'm sure Anna will be delighted when I tell her you're here."

He frowned. "I'd rather you didn't mention seeing me. Not just yet."

"Why not?"

"It would be better if you didn't. I don't want to spoil her vacation."

"But—oh. You want to surprise her when she returns?"

He inclined his head, not exactly an answer. "I would appreciate it if you don't mention me to anyone. I can't explain now, but I assure you, my reasons are valid."

Bailey wondered in exasperation why the man was so evasive. "Anna and Dean won't be back for another two and a half weeks—which you would have known if you'd bothered to call."

"Then I'll wait."

She studied him curiously. "You have that much time to blow?"

"Blow?" he repeated, looking puzzled.

"Waste."

"I won't be spending the entire time here, twiddling my thumbs," he answered wryly. "But, as it happens, I have more than enough time to, er, blow."

"What do you do? For a living, I mean."

He lifted one shoulder. "I'm very versatile."

His shrug drew her attention to his clothing. He wore a black woven shirt, buttoned to the throat, and a loosely constructed suit of a dark charcoal fabric that might have been wool or flannel. The cut was odd, rather retrospective. But it looked great on him. Anything would.

He'd worn dark colors the last time she'd seen him, she remembered. Maybe even this same suit. She wondered where he was staying, and how long he intended to stay. Before she could ask, he changed the subject.

"Anna mentioned that your brother was married before. That his first marriage ended in divorce."

Taking the comment as criticism, Bailey scowled, immediately going to her brother's defense again and forgetting the questions she'd intended to ask Bran. Which might well have been his intention, she thought, even as she burst into speech.

"Dean's first wife was a selfish witch. Gloria thinks the whole world revolves around her and her needs. When she and Dean were dating, she put on a front of being interested in his life, but after they were married, she dropped any pretense of caring about anything but herself. Nothing he could do was good enough for her, and God knows he tried to make her happy. When he realized that he was wasting his time, he stopped trying. That's when she dumped him . . . though, if you ask me, it's the best thing that could have happened to him."

"Did he move here to get away from her?"

"No. He moved here because he saw the inn advertised in a real-estate magazine and he liked the sound of it. He was bored and restless in the monotonous work routine he'd established in Chicago, and he'd always liked the idea of owning an inn. Our grandfather, Aunt Mae's father, was a hotelier. Did Anna tell you that?"

"No. She didn't."

"He had a little chain of hotels based in Atlanta. He sold them when Dean and I were young, but Dean was always interested in the business. When he saw the ad for this inn, he decided to give it a try. It wasn't quite as impulsive as it sounds, but he took a lot of people by surprise. Still, I don't think he'll ever regret his decision. This is a wonderful place."

"Yes," Bran agreed, and Bailey wondered if she imagined the wistfulness that seemed to briefly cross his face. He was expressionless again when he said, "Your former sister-in-law sounds like a difficult woman. I hope your brother is aware of how fortunate he is to have found Anna."

"He is. And Anna knows how lucky she is to have found Dean."

Bran chuckled, and Bailey was struck by how different his face looked when he smiled. Younger. Warmer. A little softer.

Devastating.

"You are very loyal to your brother, aren't you?" he asked, sounding amused by her defensiveness.

"I love him," Bailey answered simply. "Our parents died when I was six and he was fourteen. He and Aunt Mae were all the family I had after that. The three of us have been very close ever since. There's nothing I wouldn't do for either of them—or they for me."

"Then you are all very fortunate," Bran murmured, and this time Bailey knew she wasn't imagining the hint of longing in his voice. He suddenly looked very much alone, his eyes shuttered, his longish hair tumbling onto his forehead, his hands buried in the pockets of his dark slacks.

Typically, her first reaction was a desire to help him. Before, he'd been a suspicious stranger. Now that she knew he was Anna's brother, she felt some of her doubts fading. Anna wouldn't miss him so much if she didn't love him, would she? And she wouldn't love him if he hadn't in some way earned her affection. Maybe there was something Bailey could do to help.

"Would you like to sit down?" she invited, motioning toward one of the two armchairs arranged in front of the tiny fireplace that had not yet been used. "I'll make coffee."

"No coffee for me," he said. "I can't stay."

"Then sit for a minute, and we'll talk," she said, moving toward one of the chairs and settling into it invitingly. "We're family now," she added. "We should get to know each other, don't you think?"

Bran perched gingerly on the edge of the other chair, looking prepared to leave at any moment. Bailey wondered why the man was so skittish.

"Tell me about yourself," she prompted. "Where do you live? Are you married?"

That last question had just occurred to her. For some reason, she didn't like it.

It was the only one he answered. "No, I'm not married."

She tried again. "I suppose you grew up in London, like Anna? Yet I've noticed that neither of you has much of a British accent."

He shrugged. "We've moved around."

"Anna doesn't talk much about her past."

"The present is all that matters to us," he replied.

"Was your childhood an unhappy one?" Bailey asked sympathetically.

"Not particularly."

Bailey was growing more frustrated by the moment, and she could tell that he knew it, darn him.

"What *do* you do for a living?" she asked.

He hesitated. "I'm unemployed at the moment."

She sighed. "That makes two of us," she muttered.

His eyebrow rose. "You, too?"

She nodded glumly. "I was fired from my job with a large antique store in Chicago. I haven't even told my family yet, it's just too humiliating."

"Why were you fired?"

"I spoke my mind once too often."

His mouth crooked into a one-sided smile. "Why doesn't that surprise me?"

She made a face. "I can't imagine. But, really, Quentin—my ex-boss—is a jerk. He's running what could have been a great business into the ground with his stupid, impractical ideas. You can't imagine how frustrating it is to watch someone destroy a thriving business through sheer incompetence."

"Oh, I think I can imagine how you must have felt," Bran murmured, and something in his eyes told Bailey that he understood completely.

"You've had a similar experience?" she asked carefully.

He nodded, but didn't elaborate. "What will you do now?"

"I don't know. I don't think I'll move back to Chicago. I like it there, but my family is here now. I'd like to find something that will allow me to live closer to them.

There are quite a few antiques stores in Hot Springs and Little Rock. I don't know if I have the nerve, and I certainly lack the financing, to go into competition with them on my own, but maybe I could go to work for one of the larger stores as a buyer."

"Is that what you want to do? Work for someone else again? Buy and sell old furniture?"

"I love old furniture. The craftsmanship, the styles, the history. As for working for someone else—well, most people have to, don't they? Surely all bosses can't be like Quentin."

And then she realized they were talking about her, which wasn't what she wanted at all. "When was the last time you saw your sister?" she asked abruptly.

"We saw each other not long before she married your brother. Why?"

"Do you know she's expecting a baby?"

It occurred to her after she asked that Anna might have liked to have broken that news, herself. She issued her sister-in-law a mental apology, but knew she would add, in her own defense, that making conversation with Bran wasn't exactly an easy task. She found herself saying things just to get a response out of him.

"Is she?"

Bailey noted that he didn't look particularly surprised. "You already knew?"

"She must be very happy about it," he commented, neatly avoiding her question. "Anna has always wanted children."

"She and Dean are both thrilled. So am I. I can't wait to be an aunt. And you'll be an uncle. Won't that be fun?"

Bran seemed to be more interested in her. "Wouldn't you like to have children of your own?"

She felt her cheeks grow warm. Avoiding his gaze, she imitated his careless shrug. "Sure, someday. But I'm the old-fashioned type. I'd prefer to be married before I have a child. And it doesn't look as though that's going to happen anytime soon."

"Why not?"

His bluntness took her aback. "Well, it just . . . I don't know. I haven't met the right guy yet."

"How old are you?"

"I'm twenty-nine. How old are you?" she asked wryly.

"I have celebrated my twenty-fifth birthday," he replied carefully.

She lifted an eyebrow at his odd wording. "Then you're younger than I am."

He smiled then. "Not exactly." Before she could demand to know what he meant by his teasing, he spoke again. "I would have thought you'd already be married and have children by now. Most women do so by your age, don't they?"

"I think you're even more old-fashioned than I am."

He smiled. "Quite likely," he murmured.

He had a decidedly strange sense of humor. Bailey couldn't follow him at all. "You've never been married?" she asked, trying to lead the topic back to him.

"No. You're a very attractive woman, Bailey. I wouldn't have thought you'd lack for suitors."

She choked. "And you accused *me* of being outspoken!"

"I'm sorry. Have I offended you?"

"No," she admitted. "I'm not easily offended. And it isn't as though I haven't dated. It just never seemed to work out for me, relationship-wise. The guys I date all seem to have some sort of emotional baggage to deal with, and—"

"Emotional baggage?" Bran repeated, looking confused.

"Surely you've heard the term. It refers to emotional scars—you know, garbage left over from past experiences."

"I see," he said slowly. "And all the men you've dated were scarred?"

"That's an odd way to put it, but—well, yeah. I guess most of them were. I'd do my best to help them, and then, as soon as they got their confidence back, they'd move on to someone who didn't know them as well as I did by then. It seemed to embarrass them that I knew their weaknesses."

"Perhaps you've been dating the wrong sort of men."

"Obviously. But it isn't going to happen again. I'm out of the meddling, ego-bolstering business for good. Folks can just solve their own problems from now on. I—darn it, you're doing it again!"

"Doing what?" he asked blandly.

"Changing the subject. I want to talk about you."

He smiled, a slight curve of his lips that sent a warm ripple of response coursing through Bailey's middle. She swallowed.

"I find you so much more interesting," he said.

She gave him a look of reproval. "Tell me what happened between you and Anna," she said, deciding she could be as blunt as he was. "She seemed so unhappy when she mentioned you. Did you quarrel? Is there anything I can do to help?"

His smile faded. He cocked his head and spoke coolly. "Are you rummaging through *my* baggage now, Bailey?"

Her cheeks burned. "I'm just trying to help," she muttered.

"I thought you said you had given that up."

"Not when it comes to people I truly care about. Anna's part of my family now. I don't like seeing her unhappy."

"Neither do I," Bran assured her flatly. "If there were anything I could do to change the situation, I would. But believe me about this, Bailey. There is nothing you can do."

"I could listen," she suggested. "Maybe it would help if you talk about it."

"No. It wouldn't." He shifted on the chair. "I really should be going. It's very late."

"Where are you staying?"

"Not far away," he said, standing.

He glanced around the cottage, as though in curiosity. Bailey knew he noticed the lack of furnishings. There were no tables to accompany the love seat or two arm-chairs, no lamps to soften the overhead lighting, no chairs or stools pulled up to the small eating bar that separated the sitting room from the tiny, equally bare kitchenette. No prints hanging on the freshly painted walls.

"Dean hasn't had a chance to decorate this cottage yet," she said, hoping Bran wouldn't assume that the inn was as meagerly furnished. "It was finished only a few days before I arrived. I told him I'd keep my eye out for some tables and things while I'm here. I can talk to some of the local antiques dealers about a job while I'm shopping for Dean."

"Does it bother you to be out here alone?"

"It hasn't before tonight," she admitted, suddenly frowning again. "I didn't realize how easy it would be for someone to get in. How *did* you get in, Bran?"

"Make sure you check the door locks next time," he murmured.

He seemed to be implying that she'd left the front door unlocked. She bit her lip, knowing Dean would have yelled at her for such carelessness.

She must have been lulled by the comfortable rural setting of the inn, she thought. She would never have been so lax about her safety back in Chicago.

But still, Bran was hardly in a position to criticize her. "You can be sure that I will. I don't want anyone else barging in without waiting for an invitation," she said pointedly.

He acknowledged the hit with another faint smile. His dark gaze drifted downward, taking in her bare legs and feet beneath her shorts. "You aren't exactly dressed for unexpected visitors, are you? Not that I've minded the view," he added.

She stalked past him, suddenly self-conscious. She tried to hide the surge of heat that rushed through her in response to the way he'd just looked at her. It had been a long time—if ever—since she'd reacted this dramatically to a suggestive look.

"Good night, Bran," she said, twisting the dead-bolt lock to open the door. He must have locked it after he entered, she thought, though she didn't know why he would have bothered. "Next time, knock."

He was still smiling when he walked past her. Even annoyed with him, she couldn't help admiring the way he moved. The image of a sleek, silent, lethal black jungle cat popped into her mind again.

She shivered in response.

She'd always had a weakness for black cats—even the dangerous kind.

Since it was after midnight, the grounds were quiet and deserted outside the cottage. A thin fog shimmered and swirled beneath the security lighting, and a cool autumn breeze drifted in through the open door, chilling Bailey's exposed flesh.

"You'd better be careful out there," some mischievous impulse made her murmur. "Looks like a night when the ghosts could be out."

Bran seemed to stumble on the threshold. "The, er, ghosts?" he repeated huskily.

She chuckled. "Surely Anna's told you that the inn is supposedly haunted by a couple of your distant relatives who were murdered by their bootlegging stepbrother. Or at least, it was haunted until Dean and Mark released the spirits by solving their murders and redeeming the Cameron-family name."

"I haven't the faintest idea what you're talking about," Bran said, sounding a bit peevish.

"I'll have to tell you the story sometime. It's fascinating."

"It sounds ridiculous."

"Somehow I would have expected that reaction from you," Bailey said a little too sweetly. "You seem much too unimaginative to believe in ghosts."

With that, she shut the door firmly behind him. He'd deserved that after breaking into her cottage, scaring her half to death, then refusing to tell her anything about himself, even when she'd finally resorted to blatant prying.

As far as helpful meddling went, she hadn't been particularly successful that day, she thought with a rueful grimace. Neither Cara nor Bran had cooperated with her efforts to assist them.

Maybe it was time for "Dear Bailey" to concentrate on her own problems.

IT WAS ALMOST DAWN. Outside, the sky was a rich, deep purple, the sun still just a hint of brightness toward the east. A few birds chattered in the autumn-bare limbs of the trees, undisturbed by human intruders at this early hour.

Inside the cottage, the silence was disturbed only by Bailey's even breathing as she slept soundly, blissfully unaware that she wasn't alone.

Ian stood beside the bed, his hands buried in his pockets, his gaze locked on Bailey's sleep-softened face.

She'd kicked off the covers, exposing her long, shapely legs. Her T-shirt had twisted around her, baring a couple of inches of slender midriff. Her copper-tinted brown hair was tousled, one lock resting enticingly on her cheek, temptingly close to her parted lips. He longed to reach out and stroke the lock away from her face.

Would he be able to touch her? Feel her?

Anna had once described the sensation of touching Dean; it was as though she were doing it through unresponsive, unsatisfying layers of cloth, she'd said. It was that possibility that made Ian resist the impulse to reach out to Bailey.

It was better to fantasize about how warm and soft she would feel than to be confronted with a cruel reminder that he wasn't meant to touch her at all.

He knew now what made her unhappy. Though she'd recounted her problems lightly enough, he'd been able to see how badly her confidence had been shaken by her string of misfortunes in Chicago. It must be difficult for a woman who prided herself on helping others to admit she had problems of her own that she didn't know how to solve.

He smiled wryly as he remembered how confidently she'd informed him that she was out of the "meddling business," and had then proceeded to probe into what she believed to be his unhappy relationship with his sister.

Her propensity for prying was going to get her into trouble someday. Maybe he could convince her that it would be safer for her to concentrate on her own needs and let others take care of themselves.

If, of course, he ever had a chance to speak with her again.

He still feared that their two conversations thus far had been mere chance, that he would not be granted the opportunity again. Several times during the past few days, he'd been close to her without being able to reach her. With each moment he spent watching her, he grew more fascinated. She was the most intriguing woman he'd ever encountered.

He'd begun to accept that the conversation in the gazebo had been a one-time-only opportunity—one he hadn't handled at all well—and then she'd opened her bedroom door and spoken to him as he stood in her sitting room, wishing he could talk to her again.

Would she see him now if she opened her eyes? Or would he be as invisible to her as he'd been so many other occasions?

She wouldn't like knowing he was here, watching her as she slept. Yet he found himself reluctant to leave. Only when he was near her did he feel...anything. It was both pleasure and torture to be with her, knowing how truly far apart they were. Imagining how she would react if she knew the truth about him.

Often during the past years he'd chafed against the restrictions of the half life he was trapped in, but now he found himself more disheartened than ever. Bailey Gates was an all-too-vivid reminder of what he was missing. She was beautiful, bright, impulsive, kindhearted, unpredictable . . . everything he could have wanted in a woman of his own.

His gaze moved from her sleep-flushed face to the pulse that throbbed in the hollow of her throat, that visible evidence of the difference between them. He studied the rise and fall of her breasts beneath the pink T-shirt, and he imagined how they might feel against his palms. Her waist was so small he could span it with his hands, and her hips flared with a soft womanliness that made him ache to be cradled against them. Her long legs would lock neatly around him, her fingers would slide into his hair . . .

He closed his eyes and swallowed a groan.

He'd forgotten how it felt to ache like this. He'd forgotten how pleasure could so closely border pain. But even the discomfort was almost welcome after years of weary numbness.

At least he would have this to remember when Bailey was gone, when he'd returned to the anesthetic grayness.

Reluctantly, he noticed the slight tugging that would take him away until the next time he could return, whenever that might be. He hated having no control, no choice. He hated the loneliness, the meaninglessness, the hopelessness.

He opened his eyes and looked longingly at Bailey, the symbol of everything he wanted and could never have. "Bailey," he murmured, reaching out to her despite his reservations. "Ah, Bailey, I wish..."

He was taken from her before his unsteady fingers could touch her cheek.

BAILEY STIRRED against the pillows, frowning as she struggled to awaken. Had someone said her name?

Blinking against the pale light just creeping through the curtains, she peered through her tangled lashes. "Bran?" she murmured, still half-asleep. "Are you—"

A moment later, she was fully awake. And definitely alone.

Shaking her head at her foolishness, she rolled onto her side and pulled the covers up to her chin, telling herself that his voice must have come from her provocative dreams of him.

4

June 25, 1903

I met a very nice gentleman today. His name is
Gaylon Peavy and he is a widowed farmer from Sa-
line County. Esther Cunningham introduced us. His
late wife was her first cousin.

He seems quite nice. He has a young son, Charles,
who is only two years older than the twins. Charles
is a very quiet little boy, but well-behaved. Esther
tells me that Mr. Peavy is a good father.

Mr. Peavy asked several questions about the inn.
I could tell it interested him, but he was also quite
flatteringly attentive to me. He laughed at my jokes.
Mr. Carpenter never did, not that I made that many
when he was around. Thank goodness, he finally
accepted the futility of his unwelcome pursuit and
turned his attentions to Lydia Nesbitt. Her father's
general store appeals to him almost as greatly as my
inn did. And wasn't that an uncharitable thing for
me to have said? Please forgive me for my petti-
ness, diary.

Ian wasn't very well behaved during Mr. Peavy's
visit, I'm afraid. His unruly behavior was very un-
like him. I realize that he is jealous of my attention,

but I do wish he would try a little harder to be polite. Esther says a strong-willed boy needs a man's firm guidance. Perhaps she is right.

Mr. Peavy has invited me to attend the Independence Day symphony concert with him. I told him I would give him an answer as the date drew nearer, though I know it was rude of me to put him off that way. I am tempted to accept. Everyone tells me it is time to go on with my life. At least Mr. Peavy seems more likable than the others, though my heart does not beat faster when he smiles at me, the way it always did when dear James . . .

Now I've blotched the page with my tears again. How foolish of me.

I will always miss you, my darling James.

AFTER HER middle-of-the-night visit, and the spell of restlessness that followed, Bailey slept later than usual Saturday morning. It was almost eleven by the time she'd showered and dressed for the day in a simple sweater and slacks.

She glanced out the window and saw that the parking lot in front of the inn was nearly empty. The breakfast diners had already gone, and the lunch crowd had not yet arrived. She wasn't hungry, so she settled for a cup of coffee. The small electric coffeemaker was the only cooking accessory she'd requested when she'd moved in.

It was going to be another nice afternoon, though the weatherman had predicted rain for the evening. Glancing around the cottage over the rim of her coffee mug, she thought it might be a good day to do some furniture shopping. Dean had left a list of items he wanted her to locate for him, along with a budget. She'd spotted a few likely stores in Hot Springs the day before. Maybe Aunt Mae would like to go with her and check them out.

She rinsed out her mug and headed outside, making sure she locked the cottage door behind her. She found it hard to believe she'd forgotten to lock it last night, but she doubted that Bran had a key, and there had been no sign that he'd broken in.

She still didn't quite know what to make of his unexpected visit. Though he'd claimed he wanted to ask about Anna, he'd spent little time talking about his sister.

He confused her. And he fascinated her. She was more than a bit embarrassed to remember how prominently he'd appeared in her dreams. She'd actually awakened once murmuring his name.

She was distracted from her thoughts of Bran when she noticed Cara and Casey sitting in the gazebo. "Good morning."

"Good morning," Cara replied.

"How's school going, Casey?" Bailey asked.

The little girl shrugged. "Fine, thank you," she answered with what Bailey now recognized as her characteristic reticence.

Looking more closely at the child, Bailey thought she seemed a little pale, and her blue eyes were shadowed. "Aren't you feeling well, Casey?" she asked in concern.

"Casey didn't sleep well last night," Cara explained. "She had a bad dream."

"It wasn't a bad dream," Casey insisted, sounding as though this discussion had been going on for a while. "I saw someone looking in our window. It was a man. I just didn't want to wake you up and tell you."

"Apparently, she lay awake for a long time, worrying about what she thought she saw," Cara told Bailey, her own expression deeply troubled.

Bailey turned back to Casey. "You saw a man looking in your window?"

Casey nodded emphatically. "He was big and dark and his hair was black. It was really late, when everyone was asleep."

"It must have been a bad dream," Cara repeated, looking as though she wanted very much to believe her own reassurance.

Bailey wasn't so sure. Casey looked serious, and genuinely frightened. "What time was it when you saw the man, sweetie?"

"I don't know. I couldn't see a clock. But it was after midnight."

Bailey bit her lip, wondering if she should mention that she'd had a late visitor, too. After all, Bran *had* been out after midnight. And he did fit Casey's description of a tall, dark man. But he wouldn't have been peering into the windows of the inn. Why would he?

She couldn't imagine that Bran was the type of man who'd creep around peering into windows for any reason. Maybe he'd simply been passing Casey's room when she'd spotted him. That made sense—except that he wouldn't have walked past the back of the inn on the way from the cottage to the parking lot. And it couldn't have been anyone else, could it? Bailey was sure she'd finally gotten away from Larry, but . . .

"Maybe you *were* dreaming, Casey," she said gently. "Your mother's probably right. As well-lit as this place is, it would be difficult for a trespasser to sneak around without someone seeing him."

She couldn't help thinking that Bran had entered the cottage without being seen or heard by anyone but her, and he'd already been inside by the time she'd realized she wasn't alone. If he *had* been a burglar or a rapist or a stalker...well, she didn't even want to think about that.

Casey didn't look particularly comforted by Bailey's words, but she nodded politely.

"Cara, I've been looking for you. Elva told me she thought I'd find you out here."

Bailey turned in response to her aunt's voice, finding Mae coming briskly down the walkway, wearing a jade and peacock blue pantsuit and an equally bright smile. "Good morning, Aunt Mae."

"Good morning, Bailey. Did you sleep well?"

Bailey murmured an evasive reply.

"Do you need me for something, Mrs. Harper?" Cara asked, gently reminding Mae of her opening words.

"Oh, yes. You have a telephone call."

Cara's eyelashes fluttered, the only sign of her reaction to the announcement. "Mark?"

Mae nodded, her face carefully expressionless, though her eyes twinkled behind her glasses. "He says he wants to ask where you bought that scarf you were wearing the other night. He wants to get one like it for his sister's birthday."

Cara sighed. "I suppose he's holding for me."

"Yes. I told him you were here. You didn't want me to take a message, did you?" Mae asked with poorly feigned innocence.

Cara shook her head and rose, looking resigned. "I'll talk to him."

"May I talk to him, too, Mommy?" Casey asked hopefully, tagging along at her mother's side. "I want to tell him I got an *A* on my book report yesterday. He said he wanted me to let him know how I did."

"You may tell him," Cara murmured. "But, Casey— there's no need to mention your bad dream, is there?"

Casey nodded somberly. "I'll just tell him about my book report."

Bailey and Mae both watched mother and daughter walk away.

Mae exhaled lightly. "Poor Mark. He just won't give up. The scarf was only an excuse, of course. And not a very good one, at that. He's done better."

"He'll ask her out again?"

"Yes. And she'll turn him down again. I swear, I don't know which of them to feel sorrier for."

"I don't know why one of them doesn't put an end to this. If Cara isn't interested, she should tell him once and for all to stop asking her out. And you'd think Mark would finally give her an ultimatum or something. I wouldn't have any patience with all these months of the same old routine."

Mae chuckled. "No, you wouldn't. But then, you've always been one to tackle problems head-on, Bailey. You got that from me, I guess."

Bailey winced, thinking of how cowardly she'd been about even acknowledging her own problems recently, much less doing anything to solve them. "Er, Aunt Mae—"

Her aunt's attention had already moved on to something else. "I need to run into town this afternoon to have my blood-pressure medicine refilled. Would you like to go with me, dear? We could have lunch at the diner. The food's only passable, but I thought it would be a nice break from eating here three times a day."

"Sure. I was going to ask if you wanted to come shopping with me this afternoon, anyway. I told Dean I would look for some tables for the cottage as well as a few other pieces for the inn. The place really does need some accent pieces."

"That sounds like fun. When can you be ready?"

"I just have to get my purse."

"Me, too. Meet you in fifteen minutes?"

Bailey nodded and hurried back to the cottage, digging in her pocket for the key. She was about to step inside when she thought she saw a movement from the corner of her eye.

She looked toward the edge of the grounds, which were surrounded by thick woods that blocked the view of the nearest neighbors, over a quarter of a mile down the road. An old caretaker's shack—the scene of the now-legendary Cameron-twin murders—had once stood at the very edge of the woods, but Dean had torn down the remains of the building a few months ago, leaving a fresh pile of dirt in its place.

It was in that direction that she thought she'd seen someone moving around. But at second glance, she only saw trees, scraggly bushes and the posts for the privacy and security fence Dean was having constructed along the inn's grounds.

She shook her head and opened the cottage door, telling herself that she must have been more affected by the account of Casey's bad dream than she'd realized. She seemed to be unusually jumpy these days. She felt as if her past was coming back to haunt her.

THE MAN IN THE WOODS saw everything. He knew the schedules of everyone at the inn, their routines, their habits. He knew when they were together. And when they were alone.

When *she* was alone.

He waited.

When the time was right, he'd know.

And so would she.

THE SMALL TOWN of Destiny, Arkansas, had changed since the first time Bailey had visited there with Dean a year ago. The new Destiny Library was the first thing she saw when she drove down the main street. Originally named the Charles Peavy Memorial Library when it opened in January, it had been renamed a few weeks later when Mark Winter had published an article proving that the late Charles Peavy had murdered the Cameron twins and at least two others in 1921.

Mayor Charles Peavy Vandover, grandson of the murderous Charles, had borne up well under the scandal of the revelation, keeping his head high and proclaiming that he could not be held responsible for the nefarious actions of his ancestor. His cousins, Chief of Police Roy Peavy and State Representative Gaylon Peavy, had followed suit, claiming embarrassment about the story but maintaining their distance from their grandfather's deeds.

The murderer's daughter, Margaret Peavy Vandover, once the reigning grande dame of Destiny, had all but gone into seclusion during the past months. Rumor had it that she was in poor health.

The townspeople hadn't turned on the Peavys, who had contributed a great deal to the community during the past seventy-five years. Few could claim that all their own ancestors had been models of propriety—and, as Dean ruefully pointed out, money and power still had a slight edge over old-fashioned concepts like honor and justice.

The early interest in the story had waned when a lightning-ignited fire had burned down the old redbrick post office in the center of town, taking a couple of other old buildings with it and necessitating a major renovation of the downtown business section. A seventy-five-year-old scandal could hardly compete with the excitement of all the new insurance-financed construction going on in town.

Bailey could see that Dean was slowly making a place for himself here. His inn had become a popular dining spot, and the tourists he'd drawn to the area were warmly welcomed by the local shop owners who'd been struggling to survive.

Having the inn occupied again, after six years of its sitting empty, had gone a long way toward dispelling the old ghost rumors that Dean had found so disturbing when he'd first bought the inn. He'd told Bailey that he was content to let the legend fade into oblivion.

At first, some of the locals had wanted to talk to Anna about the tragic fate of her distant cousins, and some had found it compelling that fate had brought another Cameron to live in the old place again, but neither Anna nor Dean had encouraged speculation about her suspiciously timed appearance. They seemed content to leave the past alone, and concentrate on the future.

"Why do you suppose Dean and Anna are so evasive about how they met?" Bailey asked Mae over lunch in the no-frills Destiny Diner, where brightly colored Halloween cutouts served as the most prominent concession to decorating. "I've yet to hear a satisfactory explanation. First thing any of us knew, they were head over heels in love and engaged to be married."

An odd expression crossed Mae's face. "I'm sure they have their reasons for keeping the details to themselves."

"Do you think it had anything to do with Anna's family? Her brother, maybe?" Bailey asked, knowing she was coming precariously close to breaking her promise to Bran. But she couldn't help herself. She was over-whelmingly curious about him.

Mae choked on a sip of ice tea. She hastily raised a paper napkin to her lips. "Her brother?" she asked a moment later.

Bailey nodded. "I overheard Anna talking about him," she confessed. "She seemed very upset about him, as though they'd quarreled or had been separated against their will. Do you know what happened between them?"

"No," Mae replied without quite meeting Bailey's eyes. "I can't say that I do. I'm sure Anna would tell us if she wanted us to know," she added with gentle reproval.

Bailey sighed. "I know. I'm prying. But I can't help wondering . . . oh, never mind."

"Why don't we talk about you, dear? When are you going to tell me what happened in Chicago to upset you so?"

Bailey winced. She had come by her inquisitive nature honestly. Aunt Mae had raised her, after all. But she'd put this off for as long as she could. It was time to come clean.

She drew a deep breath. "I called Quentin a pompous, pretentious fraud who wouldn't know quality antiques from do-it-yourself furniture kits. I told him I was tired of covering for him, tired of working sixteen-hour days seven days a week, tired of kissing up to his obnoxious clients and being treated in return like a lowly peasant. I said he could either start treating me with the respect I deserve or he could fire me."

"He fired you," Mae said, and it wasn't a question.

Bailey nodded. "He fired me."

"Best thing that could have happened to you, if you ask me."

"You're probably right. But it still stung. I worked hard for that man. For him to just throw me away like that..."

"You deserve better, Bailey. And you'll find it."

Bailey stirred her coffee, though she hadn't put any milk or sugar in it. "I hope you're right."

"I'm right. Now tell me about Larry."

Bailey groaned. "You're determined to hear the whole ugly tale, aren't you?"

"How bad is it?"

Bailey looked away. "Bad."

"Bailey..." Quick concern colored Mae's voice.

She shook her head. "It's all right. I took care of it. I just...well, I thought I was a better judge of character than that."

"It's not a flaw to want to believe the best of people, dear," Mae said gently. "You just have to learn to be careful."

Bailey wondered what her aunt would say if she knew the whole truth about Larry—or about Bran. Bailey had hardly been careful where Bran was concerned, even when she'd found him inside her cottage without her permission. Obviously, he was a troubled man, a loner who couldn't reach out even to his own sister. There was a lost, haunted look in his eyes that tugged at her, at the same time as something about him warned her to keep her distance.

Without knowing anything about him—what he did, where he'd been, even where he was staying—Bailey had agreed to keep his presence a secret. She'd been alone with him on two occasions, and would probably be again, if he came back. She couldn't turn him away, and not only because he was Anna's brother. Somehow during the course of those two brief interludes with him, it had become more personal than that.

She really was an idiot.

"Bailey?" Mae sounded as though she'd spoken more than once without getting a response.

Bailey blinked. "Sorry, Aunt Mae. I was just... thinking."

She tried to push thoughts of Bran to the back of her mind. She wouldn't mention him yet, but she made herself a promise that she was going to be more careful from now on. Despite her abysmal record, she was determined to learn from her mistakes.

Just then, a portly, pleasant-looking man with rather squinty brown eyes stopped by the table on his way past. "Hey, there, Miz Harper. How's everything out at the inn?"

"Fine, thank you, Mr. Cooley. Have you met my niece?"

The man smiled broadly at Bailey. "Don't believe I've had the pleasure."

"Bailey, this is R. J. Cooley, Dean's insurance agent. Mr. Cooley, Bailey is Dean's sister."

"Real nice to meet you, ma'am," Cooley said, enthusiastically pumping Bailey's hand. "You visiting or are you moving to this area yourself?"

"Just visiting for now."

"You should think about moving here, like your brother and your aunt. It's a great place to live. My family's been in these parts for a long time."

The talkative salesman went on to describe his family history in lengthy detail. Sharing a smile over the table, Bailey and Mae feigned interest.

Actually, Bailey was relieved that the conversation no longer centered on her own history.

BAILEY PUT A HAND to the back of her neck, tilted her head and winced as her muscles clenched. For the past hour and a half, she'd been hunched over a laptop computer that she'd borrowed from Dean's office, working on her résumé.

Lacking a desk or table in the cottage, she'd been sitting cross-legged on the bed, the computer in front of her—not exactly an ergonomically desirable position, she admitted. She decided she'd better take a break before her entire body locked in protest.

She pushed the computer aside without turning it off and swung her bare legs over the edge of the bed. She was wearing a loose-fitting knit shorts-set again, her favorite lounging and sleeping apparel. The new carpeting was thick and soft beneath her bare feet. She dug in her toes and stretched luxuriously, shaking the stiffness out of her arms.

Her eyes still closed, she bent to touch her toes. Something tickled her right foot. She opened her eyes to find a large brown spider sitting on top of her foot, inches from her nose.

Bailey let out a scream that should have shattered all the windows in the cottage. A second later, she was standing in the middle of the bed, trembling, and the spider was cowering in one corner of the bedroom.

"Bailey! What is it? What frightened you?"

The deep voice from the doorway was the most welcome sound she'd ever heard.

"Bran!" she gasped, still breathless from her shock. "It's a spider. It's huge and it was on my foot. Oh, ugh, I *hate* spiders."

He'd looked poised for battle when she'd spotted him in the doorway. Now he relaxed, looking at her in disbelief. "A spider? You let out a scream like that over a spider?"

"I told you, I hate spiders," she answered defensively. "And it's a big one. It's over there. In that corner."

Bran followed the direction of her pointing, unsteady finger. "That's a grass spider. They're harmless."

"I don't care. I want it out of here. Please, would you kill it or something?"

"No."

She stared at him, trying to read his suddenly expressionless face. "You won't do *anything*?"

"It won't hurt you, Bailey. Besides, it's gone now. Look for yourself."

Cautiously, she glanced toward the corner. It was empty. There was no sign of the eight-legged intruder.

Resentfully, she turned back to the two-legged one. "Now we don't know where it is. It could be lurking somewhere just waiting for me to walk barefoot across the floor again."

"I'm sure that spider is trying to get as far away from you as physically possible," Bran contended. "It had to be more frightened than you were. Has anyone ever mentioned that you have a bloodcurdling scream?"

Bailey blushed. "Yes. Dean has told me I could wake the dead with it."

Bran cleared his throat. "Very likely."

"Sorry, it's just that when I saw the thing on my foot, I—hey, wait a minute. What are you doing in my bedroom? Darn it, you've done it again. Waltzed right in without knocking or anything."

"When I heard you scream, I thought you needed help. I didn't think there was time to wait for an invitation."

"You're telling me I left the front door unlocked again?" She thought she'd locked it, but she'd been carefully carrying Dean's computer when she'd entered, which must have distracted her. She really was going to have to be more cautious, she reminded herself.

Bran tilted his head. "Are you going to stand up there all night?"

Her blush deepened. She must look like a fool, standing in the middle of the bed with her tousled hair and bare feet. Bran, on the other hand, looked as elegant and immaculate as ever. She did wonder, however, if he owned any clothing other than that dark shirt and suit.

She climbed carefully off the bed, keeping one eye out for spiders. "I was just going to have a cola," she said with hastily reclaimed dignity. "Can I get you anything?"

"No. Thank you."

She moved toward him. He remained in the doorway, blocking her path out of the room. She paused only inches from where he stood, and looked up at him uncertainly. He was watching her with that shuttered, inscrutable expression, his dark eyes fixed on hers with an intensity that took her breath away.

She thought she saw a quick flare of desire cross his face, and she felt an answering flame ignite somewhere deep inside her. Bran backed away before she could be entirely sure of what had passed between them.

She took her time in the kitchenette, pouring a diet soda over ice. She needed that moment to regain her composure. When she turned around, Bran wasn't in the sitting room where she'd expected him to be. Frowning, she went in search of him.

He was in the bedroom, standing beside the bed. Hands in his pockets, he studied the glowing screen of the portable computer, a puzzled expression on his face. "What is this?"

"I'm working on my résumé. I thought I'd start sending it out next week."

"I was talking about this device. What do you call it?"

"Haven't you ever seen a laptop computer before? Or is this one called a notebook? I can't remember all the terms, the technology changes so quickly."

Bran shook his head. "What does it do?"

She wondered if he was putting her on. "Everything a bigger computer does. C'mon, Bran, you must have used a computer before. Everyone born in this century has surely been exposed to one at some point or another."

He lifted his head, looking rather offended by her skepticism. "Never mind." He turned away from the computer before she could decide whether she should apologize—or figure out why.

His attention zeroed in on the slim brown covered book lying on top of the chest of drawers. "Where did you find this?" he asked without touching the book.

"In that box," she replied, nodding toward the corner. "Aunt Mae found it in the attic of the inn and asked me to look through the books in it. So far, I've only glanced at the ones on top. They look old, but I haven't seen anything of particular value."

Bran seemed fascinated by the little brown book. His hand lifted, as though to pick it up, then fell to his side. "This looks like a child's storybook," he commented with a touch of gruffness.

"It is. Bedtime stories. I've been reading them—or trying to. The pages are in poor condition. I found your name in there."

He looked quickly around at her. "*My* name?"

She nodded. "It's a story about Prince Bran of Ireland. He sailed the southern seas and returned home a hundred years later, still a handsome young man. Do you know the tale?"

"Yes, my mother liked it," he answered slowly. "She'd heard it as a child from her own mother."

"Is that where you got your name?"

"Yes."

He looked again at the book, and Bailey wondered at the expression in his eyes. Sadness? Nostalgia? Longing?

"You're welcome to look at it, if you like," she urged, wishing she could understand this mysterious, complex man.

But he'd already turned away from the book, his expression closed again. "I should go," he said.

"Don't go yet," Bailey protested automatically. "Can't you stay and talk for a few minutes?"

He eyed her warily. "What do you want to talk about?"

"About you," she answered, exasperated. "Bran, I know nothing about you. Why did you come by tonight? Where are you staying? What's going on between you and Anna?"

He surprised her with a faint smile. "You really are the curious sort, aren't you?"

"Yes, I am. Compulsively," she admitted frankly. "And, to be quite honest, you are driving me crazy."

His smile deepened. "Am I?"

Oh, heavens, when he smiled . . .

Bailey resisted an impulse to fan her warm face with her free hand. "I wish you would tell me something about yourself."

His smile faded. "There's little to tell."

"Somehow, I find that very hard to believe."

"There are many things about me that you would probably find very hard to believe."

It was enough to drive a sober woman to drink. Bailey took a calming gulp of her soda, then abruptly set the glass on the dresser. "You," she said as calmly as she could manage, "are the most frustrating, uncooperative, secretive, annoying man I have ever met."

He didn't smile, though his eyes warmed with what looked like private amusement. He moved closer to her, his voice lowering to a sexy growl. "And you are the most inquisitive, most generous and most intriguing woman I have ever known," he replied. "You also have the most beautiful legs I've ever seen."

She promptly went scarlet. "You're only trying to distract me," she said, suddenly self-conscious of wearing her shorts.

"I'm being completely truthful," he countered. "Isn't that what you wanted?"

"Not about my legs," she protested.

"Would you prefer that I talk about your beautiful blue eyes? Or your lovely, warm smile? Or your musical voice or slender waist or full, soft—"

"No," she said in a choked voice, holding up a hand to stop him. "I don't think you need to mention any of those things."

Even though she couldn't help being flattered that he'd noticed.

"We were talking about you," she reminded him somewhat desperately.

"No," he said gently, his gaze focused on her hand, which hovered only an inch or so away from his chest. "*You* were talking about me. I find you much more interesting."

She suddenly wanted to touch him. To be touched by him. It was foolish, but the urge was almost overwhelming. She lifted her hand toward his face. "Bran, I—"

He jerked out of her reach just as the telephone on the nightstand shattered the intimacy between them with a demanding ring.

Bailey stood with her hand suspended in midair, wondering why Bran had acted as though her touch would burn him. Why he was still looking at her as though she was dangerous.

The telephone rang again, insistently.

"You should answer that," Bran said after a moment.

She nodded and moved to pick up the receiver. "Hello."

"Hi, Bailey, it's Dean. How are you?"

"Dean," she repeated, her eyes still focused on Bran. "I'm fine. Are you and Anna enjoying your vacation?"

"Yes, we're having a wonderful time. Anna sends her love."

"Give my love to her."

"I must go," Bran murmured, just loudly enough for Bailey to hear. "Please don't mention me."

She nodded numbly, watching as he turned and disappeared through the bedroom door and into the other room.

"Bailey?" Dean urged.

She turned her attention back to the call, managing to carry on a reasonably coherent conversation with her brother. She kept her promise to Bran; she didn't mention him to Dean. She wasn't sure exactly what she would have said about him, anyway.

The call didn't last long. Dean had simply wanted to check in with her, to ask if she was comfortable in the cottage, to make sure she was all right. When she hung up, she walked into the sitting room, only to find it empty. The front door was securely locked.

Bran had left as silently as he'd arrived.

Bailey sank wearily onto the couch, suddenly feeling very much alone.

THE SILENCE was absolute. Not even the faintest whisper of sound disturbed it.

The grayness was cold. Sterile. Empty.

Ian stood alone in the middle of nowhere, his hands in his pockets, his shoulders hunched in misery.

The isolation was the worst part of his existence. The constant uncertainty of when—if ever—he would leave this place again.

When—if ever—he would see Bailey again.

After her first encounter with Dean, Anna had learned to come and go from this place almost at will. Ian had been trying ever since to duplicate that feat, with no success. He seemed to be whisked back and forth by some unseen force with a purpose of its own. One moment he would be here, the next there. Sometimes Bailey could see him, other times she couldn't.

He hated it.

If he closed his eyes, he could picture her, looking at him with such lively curiosity and honest compassion, and an attraction she probably thought she concealed. He could still see her hand, reaching out to touch him. He'd been so tempted to let her . . .

How would she feel if she knew she had almost touched a dead man?

He opened his eyes and slammed his right fist into his left palm, wishing there was something more solid upon which to take out his frustrations.

The silence was unbroken.

5

December 23, 1902

Two days until Christmas. The children are so excited. The decorations we've hung around the inn are lovely. I must confess, the holiday spirit has overtaken me, as well.

I hope the twins will like their gifts. I bought Ian a set of toy soldiers and a bag of marbles. I found Mary Anna the most beautiful dark-haired doll, which has two dresses and a little crib. Mary Anna so loves playing with her "babies." She will adore this one.

My favorite of their gifts is the storybook I discovered in a bookstore in Hot Springs. It is a book of bedtime stories, some of the same ones my own mother read to me. It includes the story of Prince Bran, my childhood hero. I think Ian will like it.

Gaylon has become more persistent in his courting. He seems to be genuinely fond of me. He wants a wife and a mother for young Charles. He shows great interest in the inn. He says he has grown tired of farming and would like the challenge of running a business. There are many days when I would not mind turning over the responsibilities to him.

He kissed me quite passionately last evening. I didn't try to stop him. His embraces were not unpleasant, though I could not respond with the same enthusiasm I once felt for such things. The thought of being intimate with Gaylon embarrasses me, but it doesn't repulse me. He doesn't seem to mind that I am not the intensely passionate type—at least, not with him. He cannot know, of course, how different it once was for me.

I worry so about Ian. He's such a complex child. He's still very loving to me and to Mary Anna, but he's becoming so mistrustful of people outside our family. Gaylon, for instance. How I wish Ian would give poor Gaylon a chance.

Ian is being difficult. He refuses to accept Gaylon's presence in our lives. He doesn't like Charles. He won't even talk about the situation. I'm trying to be patient with him. I know this must be confusing for a six-year-old boy. But he will simply have to accept that I know what is best for us. Gaylon is being very tolerant. He says Ian will come around, given time. I hope that he is right.

I am doing the best that I can, for all of us.

BAILEY FOUND MARK sitting in one of the rockers lining the inn's front porch late the next afternoon. He looked perfectly at home there, rocking and humming and waving at the early arrivals for dinner as though he were the official host of the place.

Smiling, Bailey took a seat in the rocker next to him. "Hanging out?" she asked.

"Yeah. I like sitting here. I was the one who told Dean he should line the porch with rockers for his guests. They've had a lot of use. It's rare that I find them empty like this."

"I know. There's almost always someone out here, rocking. Good idea, Mark."

He shrugged. "Dean would have thought of it on his own, eventually. I really just wanted a place to sit and rock, myself. My apartment doesn't have a front porch."

Bailey drew a deep breath of crisp late-October air. "It's cool this afternoon, isn't it? Hard to believe it will be winter soon."

"Yeah. It doesn't usually get really cold here until late December or January, but it can get pretty nippy in November."

Having exhausted the weather as a conversational topic, Bailey moved on. "How are things at the newspaper?"

"Biggest story this week has been the busted water line on Main Street yesterday. A guy running a backhoe hit it and darn near flooded city hall."

"That *is* exciting," Bailey murmured with a smile.

"You bet. They even brought out the fire truck."

"Why did they need the fire truck?"

"They didn't, but it has to be started up every now and then. Keeps the battery from going dead."

Bailey laughed, knowing Mark was exaggerating, but enjoying his nonsense, anyway.

"Oh, yeah, and Mr. Carmette reported a trespasser. Said it looked as though the guy had been camping out on his property."

"Mr. Carmette?"

Mark nodded. "Lives on the other side of these woods, down the road about a half mile from here. He caught a glimpse of the guy late last night—said he was big and had dark hair, but that was the only description he could give. He ran into the house and got his rifle, but the man was gone by the time he got back out. He called Chief Peavy and raised hell. Mr. Carmette does not like having his privacy violated."

"Obviously not," Bailey murmured, frowning.

She couldn't help wondering about the dark-haired man who'd been spotted twice now late at night. Could it possibly have been Bran that Casey and the angry Mr. Carmette had seen?

She wouldn't have described Bran's whipcord build as big, but he was tall, which could mean the same to some. He was dark-haired. And he had been so evasive about where he was staying.

She really was going to have to get some answers about Bran soon. Before someone else started asking questions.

She changed the subject deliberately. Something about Mark's clear green eyes told her that his mild manner concealed a sharp perceptiveness that could prove inconvenient if he sensed that she was troubled about something. "Are you staying for dinner?"

He nodded. "The special tonight is meat loaf and creamed potatoes with gravy. Elva's gravy is the best I've ever tasted."

"Aunt Mae and I would love to have you join us at our table."

"Thanks. I'd like that. Er—I suppose Cara and Casey will be eating in the kitchen, as usual?"

"I'm sure they will," Bailey answered gently. "Cara says she likes to share a quiet meal with her daughter when they get the chance."

"Yeah, but it also makes a nice excuse for her to stay hidden from the guests and diners," Mark grumbled. "Not to mention me."

"When are you going to give up, Mark?" Bailey couldn't resist asking.

He shrugged. "I'm not. I can't," he answered simply. "Someday, she's going to realize she can trust me. I'm making headway, I think. She doesn't turn pale and bolt in the other direction when she sees me now."

"She isn't exactly throwing herself into your arms, either."

He groaned. "You really are Mae's niece, aren't you?"

Bailey wrinkled her nose. "I'm afraid so. Sorry."

"Don't apologize. I'm crazy about that aunt of yours. And I like you, too, Bailey Gates."

She smiled at him. "Thanks. You're not so bad yourself, Mark Winter."

Someone cleared her throat behind them. Bailey and Mark looked around to find Cara standing there, frowning at them. "Mrs. Harper wanted to know if you're ready for dinner, Bailey."

Bailey stood. "Yes, thanks, Cara. Mark will be joining us tonight. Wouldn't you and Casey like to dine with us, too?"

"Thank you, but no. We had an early dinner. Casey wants me to watch something on television with her this evening."

"Hey, how about if you and I take Casey out for ice cream or something after the program?" Mark suggested, as though on impulse.

Cara shook her head. "Tomorrow's a school day. She has to be in bed early."

"Another time, then," Mark said, seemingly unfazed.

"Perhaps," Cara murmured, then turned and walked away, leaving Mark staring wistfully after her.

Bailey slipped a hand beneath Mark's arm, her heart twisting in sympathy at the hopeless look in his eyes. She wished there was something she could do to help him—and Cara, for that matter. Both of them were obviously in a great deal of pain. Unfortunately, Bailey didn't seem to have any answers these days. For her friends—or for herself.

IAN STOOD UNSEEN at one end of the porch, his fists clenched at his sides. He hated the way Bailey smiled at Winter, hated the easy way she touched him. It was made even worse because he wanted so desperately to be touched by her, himself.

He glowered at the smiling couple, despising Mark Winter with an intensity of emotion he hadn't felt in a very long time. And knowing full well that his hostility was based on nothing more than deep, aching, burning jealousy.

As far as he knew, Winter was a decent man. And he was a good friend to Dean and Anna. He had helped prove the truth about that long-ago tragedy, even at the risk of his own career and local reputation. There had been a time when Ian had been grateful to him for what he'd done.

Now all he wanted was to make him disappear. Permanently.

Mark Winter could be with Bailey in a way that Ian could not. He could laugh with her, dine with her, be seen with her. Touch her. Hold her.

Ian closed his eyes and tilted his head backward, cursing himself for wanting what he couldn't have. Hadn't he wished for Bailey to be happy? Hadn't he wanted to see her smile? Hadn't he hoped to encourage her to go on with her life, despite her recent setbacks? Was he truly so selfish that he would begrudge her a chance to spend time with a suitable, respectable man?

Ian had nothing to offer her.

Not even himself.

How long could he go on this way? What did he have to do to bring an end to it?

Even oblivion would be preferable to this.

"ELVA DEFINITELY MAKES the best gravy I've ever eaten," Mark said in satisfaction a while later, pushing away his thoroughly emptied plate. "It's no wonder the inn is becoming the most popular place to eat around here. Before long, it's going to be necessary to make a reservation."

Mae smiled. "I'll be sure and pass your compliments on to Elva."

"You do that."

Bailey was just finishing her own dinner of grilled chicken and steamed fresh vegetables. The menu of the Cameron Inn's twenty-table dining room was limited but excellent. The selections rotated so that neither the guests nor the local diners would grow tired of the choices, and Elva was always on the lookout for a new recipe. She was particularly renowned for her desserts, especially her pies, with their "mile-high meringues."

Dean had chosen well when he'd hired his head cook. As he had with his other staff, Bailey thought in approval. She'd always known her brother would be a success at anything he put his mind to. She had no doubt that he would be as good at being a father as he was at innkeeping.

"I can't help envying Dean," she mused, hardly aware that she'd spoken aloud, her voice just audible over the cheerful clatter of the dining room.

"Why is that, dear?" Mae asked gently.

Bailey shrugged, slightly embarrassed. "Well, he's found a place for himself. A business he enjoys, a permanent home, a wife he adores. Now they're going to start a family. He's a very lucky man."

"He is that," Mark agreed, a bemused expression crossing his face. "I would say that destiny played a major role in his good fortune."

"The town, or the philosophy?" Bailey asked with a smile.

"Both," Mark replied cryptically.

"How did you end up here, Mark?" she asked.

"I worked as a political reporter in Little Rock for a few years. Then I burned out. The *Destiny Daily* was owned by a friend of my father's. When Harold decided to sell, he called me to see if I was interested. I was. My associates in Little Rock thought I'd lost my mind. They pointed out how risky it was to buy a small-town daily at a time when newspapers were folding all over the country due to heavy competition from cable-TV news. I knew a small-town daily could offer something CNN couldn't provide—local gossip. If I was to put photos of the local kids in the pages, along with stories of their accomplishments, their parents and grandparents would keep me in business."

"I've read your paper," Bailey reminded him, chiding him for his self-deprecation. "It's an excellent small-town daily. You have just the right mix of local color and national news. And your feature stories are particularly well done."

"Mark won a state press award for his article on the Cameron twins," Mae bragged.

Mark shrugged. "It was a hell of a story. Anyone who could string a sentence together would have won an award with it."

"I don't think so. I read the article," Bailey argued. "It was brilliant, Mark. You took the story of a seventy-five-year-old tragedy and made it fresh and gripping. I was crying for the poor twins long before I finished reading your account of what had happened to them, and the unwarranted damage that had been done to their reputations ever since. I felt such satisfaction that you vindicated them. You really should consider writing a book."

"Maybe I will someday," Mark murmured. "But not about that. Dean has made me promise I'd let that story drop now that we've cleared the twins' names."

Bailey wondered why Dean was so adamant about letting the story be forgotten. It really was an interesting tale. "I guess he's reluctant to involve Anna," she said.

Both Mark and Mae seemed to stiffen.

"What do you mean, Bailey?" Mae asked.

Mark only watched her, his eyes searching her face in a way that made Bailey wonder what on earth she'd said.

"I only meant that since the twins were distant relatives of hers, curious people might annoy her with a lot of questions. Or maybe Dean's afraid the inn will be invaded by a mob of New Age types hoping to contact the twins' tormented spirits or some garbage like that. Why? What did you think I meant?"

Mae and Mark exchanged a glance. To Bailey, it seemed as though they were both trying to decide how much the other knew. She wished she had even the faintest idea what lay behind their odd behavior.

Not for the first time, she had the feeling that there was something about this inn and its history that everyone knew except her. She felt very much the outsider at that moment.

Would she, like Dean, ever find a place where she truly belonged? she wondered with a wistfulness she tried to hide from her dinner companions.

Mark stayed late, talking in the sitting room with Bailey and Mae. Bailey suspected that he was hoping Cara would join them eventually, but she never did. When Mark had delayed returning to his lonely apartment as long as he could, he stood with a sigh. "Guess I'd better go."

"I'll walk you out," Bailey offered, rising. "I need to finish writing my résumé tonight."

"I hope you find a job close by," Mark said with a warm smile. "We would all enjoy having you here."

She returned the smile, knowing that her brother's friend had become hers, as well. It was nice to make new friends—whether she could help them with their problems or not.

Bailey kissed her aunt's cheek on the way out. "Good night, Aunt Mae. I'll see you tomorrow."

"Good night, dear. Don't work too late on your résumé. There's no great rush, is there?"

Bailey smiled, moved by the loving concern in her aunt's voice, a poignant reminder of her childhood. "I won't be too late," she promised.

It was starting to drizzle when Bailey and Mark walked outside, a cold mist laden with the promise of winter. Bailey burrowed into the baseball-style jacket she wore with her sweater and jeans. "The weatherman said we'd have this rain last night. Looks like they were about twenty-four hours too early."

"The weather's a lot like a woman—very hard to predict."

Bailey laughed and slid her hand beneath his arm. "The old country philosopher," she teased.

He shrugged. "Maybe I'll become the next Mark Twain."

"There's nothing wrong with being Mark Winter."

He sighed. "Tell Cara that."

"Maybe I will."

He stiffened. "I didn't mean that literally," he assured her hastily. "Don't get involved in this, Bailey. It wouldn't do any good."

"Maybe not," she said, her chin lifting stubbornly. "But someone should do something. The two of you are both so obviously miserable, it makes me itch to get involved."

"It isn't that I don't appreciate the thought, I just want to try to handle this myself, okay?"

"Fine. When were you planning to start?" she asked politely.

He sighed gustily. "Okay, I get the hint. It's time for me to change tactics, I suppose."

"It is unless you want to spend the rest of your life asking and being turned down for dates."

"I'm not sure my ego, secure as it is, can take that much longer."

"Then maybe you should sit her down for a serious talk, whether she likes it or not."

"Maybe you're right. Maybe I will. Someday. Hey— what was that?"

Bailey jerked her head in the direction he was pointing, toward the edge of the inn's property.

"I thought I saw a light over there," Mark said. "A flashlight, maybe. I don't see anything now."

Still looking hard in the direction he'd indicated, Bailey wiped a drop of rain off her nose. "I don't see anything, Mark."

He shook his head. "Neither do I now. I must have been mistaken."

"I guess you were still thinking about Mr. Carmette's trespasser."

"Maybe. Still, you lock your doors tonight, you hear?"

She chuckled ruefully. "Now you sound just like Bran."

Mark cocked his head curiously. "Bran?"

She winced. "A, er, a friend."

"Oh. C'mon, I'll walk you to your cottage."

"Don't be silly. The cottage is in the opposite direction of the parking lot. You'd get soaked walking there and back. Go on to your car. I'll make it to the cottage on my own."

"I was only trying to be chivalrous," he said with teasing sanctimony.

She smiled. "I know. And it was sweet of you. Good night, Mark."

"'Night, Bailey. Hurry inside now, or you'll catch cold."

"Go," she ordered, giving him a slight shove in the direction of the parking lot.

"I'm gone." Grinning, he turned and loped toward his car, his head bent against the light rain.

Bailey glanced once more at the woods, contented herself that there was nothing there, then headed for the cottage. Just as she reached the gazebo, the rain began to fall in earnest. She briefly debated between dashing for the cottage or ducking beneath the shelter of the gazebo.

Something made her decide on the gazebo.

The structure's open-woodwork walls provided little warmth, but the peaked roof kept her dry. Tiny decorative white bulbs lined the Victorian roof and provided soft, festive lighting. She sat on one of the built-in benches, her feet drawn up in front of her, hands locked around her knees, and watched the rain fall. Her thoughts were far away, and she was hardly conscious of the damp chill of the evening.

She was thinking of Bran. Perhaps that explained why she wasn't really surprised to hear his voice from close beside her. "You shouldn't be out here alone at night," he said.

She looked over her shoulder, saw him standing there looking at her with that dark, brooding expression of his, and she smiled. "I was waiting for you."

6

February 5, 1903

As I expected, Gaylon asked me to marry him last evening.

I haven't yet given him an answer. He says he understands that I need time to consider his proposal, though we both have known for some time that he intended to ask. He's being very patient with me.

I am greatly tempted to accept his offer. Sometimes the responsibilities I face alone are overwhelming. If I could turn over the daily operation of the inn to Gaylon, I would have more time for the children, and they do seem to need more and more of my time of late. Ian, particularly.

He isn't a bad child. Just the opposite, in fact. He loves us so deeply that he can't bear to think of anything changing. He is jealous, and feels threatened, and that makes him rather sullen, I'm afraid. He fears that Gaylon and Charles will disrupt the happy lives we have made for ourselves. I've tried to make him understand that I will have more time for him and Anna if I marry Gaylon, not less, but it is difficult for him to comprehend at his age.

I can't really tell how Mary Anna feels about the situation. She tends to parrot Ian, but she is generally more accepting of change than he is. More tolerant of the weaknesses of others. She isn't close to Gaylon, nor to Charles, but she doesn't seem to actively dislike them.

Ian asked me if I still love his father. His question broke my heart. I did not know how to explain to him that my love for James will never waver, that I still love him so desperately there are times I wonder if I can go on without him. Even after all these years alone, there is not a day that goes by that I do not miss him, or see him in our children's faces. Not a day that I don't grieve for him.

How does one explain to a child that love is not always the foundation for marriage? I have not pretended to Gaylon that I love him, though I have assured him with complete honesty that I am fond of him. He doesn't seem to mind. He told me he hopes my feelings for him will deepen with time. Perhaps he is right, though I have my doubts.

He will be a good husband to me. A father for the twins. Even for Ian, if the boy will allow it. Gaylon continues to assure me that Ian will come around when he realizes that he has no choice. I hope he is right. I couldn't bear to hurt my son when all I want is what is best for him. Everyone is urging me to accept Gaylon's proposal. Everyone says Ian needs a man's influence. They all believe it is the right thing for me to do.

If only there were some way for me to know without doubt that they are right.

Oh, James, can't you help me? Is there no sign you can give me of what you would have me do? I desperately need your guidance.

WITHOUT TAKING his eyes from Bailey's face, Ian sat on the bench, careful not to touch her. "What do you mean you were waiting for me? How did you know I would come tonight?"

She shrugged, still smiling. "I just did."

His attention focused on that gentle curve of her lips, the glimpse of white teeth between them. She had a beautiful smile. He thought of the way she'd smiled at Winter, and he scowled. "Who was your friend? The one who just left?" he asked, feigning ignorance of Mark's identity.

She tilted her head. "You saw us?"

"Yes."

"Why didn't you say something? I would have introduced you. He's a good friend of Dean and Anna's."

"You looked quite friendly with him, as well," Ian muttered, disregarding her question.

"He's a very nice man. His name is Mark Winter, and he's the editor of the local newspaper."

Ian's scowl deepened. "Oh."

"He's also very much in love with Dean's housekeeper, Cara McAlister," Bailey added deliberately.

Ian squirmed on the bench, wondering if his irrational jealousy had really been so transparent. "Is he?"

"Yes. Not that it's getting him anywhere," she added with a slight sigh. "Poor Mark."

"Why do you say that?"

"Cara isn't giving him the time of day. There are times when she seems interested—at least, to me, she does— but every time he gets close to her, she seems to put up an emotional wall. She's afraid, I think. Dean believes she's been involved in an abusive relationship, and now is wary of getting too close to anyone. That makes sense. It wouldn't be easy to trust again, especially if the guy had been a violent jerk."

Something in Bailey's voice caught Ian's attention. "You aren't speaking from personal experience, are you?"

She turned away, but he could still see her profile in the soft lighting. He saw the slight spasm that crossed her face just before she answered. "In a way."

His eyes narrowed. A wave of fury crashed through him. "You were involved with a man who used violence against you?"

He saw her swallow. "A few months ago, I dated a man who seemed nice enough. An art dealer who had a shop close to the antique store where I worked. He was really broken up about his recent divorce. I thought he needed a friend. We started dating, and things seemed to be going very well. He could be very charming—as long as things went his way."

"And when things didn't go his way?"

She grimaced. "At first, I was so eager to make him happy that everything was just great. And then, when I got involved with my own problems at work, I realized how one-sided the relationship really was. Larry didn't care about my troubles. He only needed someone to constantly bolster his own ego. When I finally understood what he was really like and broke it off with him, he sort of went nuts."

"Nuts?" Ian repeated, hearing the iciness of his own voice. Anna had once commented that the hotter his temper flared, the colder his voice became.

"You know, strange. He started stalking me. Demanding to know where I was all the time. Who I was seeing. Threatening me. It went on for a couple of months. It was too much for me to deal with on top of my unhappiness at work. One day, I just lost it. I told my boss what he could do with his attitude—and he canned me, of course. That evening, Larry showed up on my doorstep and I told him off, too. I started screaming at him and throwing things at him like a maniac.

"I told him if he ever came near me again, I would take his head off. I didn't mean it, naturally, but I was so steamed I was saying anything that popped into my mind. He wasn't used to anyone fighting back—apparently, his ex-wife was a doormat until she finally got the nerve to get away from him. Anyway, he left and I started packing, and the next day I was on a plane headed here."

Ian hadn't understood some of the terms she'd used, but the gist of her tale was clear. "If I ever see him, I'll take care of him for you. Permanently," he said quietly. He knew his threat was an empty one—there was little he could actually do to the man—but it felt good to say it.

Bailey jerked around to face him. "You would do no such thing! Honestly, Bran, you sound like a vigilante. You should know that violence is no solution to anything."

"And you should know by now that it's dangerous to get involved with other people's problems." His own, for that matter, he thought glumly.

"I told you, I've quit doing that. I learned my lesson."

Ian glanced toward the inn through the blurring curtain of rain. "What about the housekeeper and Mark Winter? Aren't you getting involved with them?"

"Well, maybe I offer a little advice, a sympathetic ear..." Her voice faded, and she grimaced self-consciously. "Okay, you're right. I should stay out of it. It's just that I hate to see people I like being unhappy."

She looked at him, and he knew the conversation had suddenly turned more personal. "You, for example," she murmured. "You seem so lonely. Why won't you let me introduce you to Aunt Mae and the others? Why do you have to wait alone for Anna?"

"I haven't been alone," he reminded her. "Not all the time. I've been with you." She couldn't possibly know how grateful he was for these too-brief moments of companionship.

She swung her feet to the floor and scooted closer to him on the bench. "It's getting colder," she said softly.

He tensed, prepared to move quickly away. "You should go inside."

"I will. In a minute. Despite the cold, it's nice out here, isn't it?"

He heard the rain on the roof of the little gazebo, and on the grounds surrounding them, muting other sounds from the inn and the almost-deserted parking lot. The tiny white lights glowed softly above them, creating a secluded island in the dark, wet night. He didn't feel the cold, but he was very aware of Bailey, sitting so close.

"It is nice," he agreed huskily. *And painful*, he could have added, but he wasn't willing to explain how much it hurt to be so close to her without being able to touch her.

"Bran, may I ask you something?"

He eyed her warily. "What?"

"Have you been camping on Mr. Carmette's property?"

"I haven't been camping on anyone's property," he assured her flatly. "I don't even know who Mr. Carmette is."

"He lives on the other side of the woods. He reported a trespasser last night."

"And you thought I was that trespasser?"

"It crossed my mind," she said with a hint of apology.

"You were mistaken."

"Casey—the housekeeper's little girl—thought she saw someone looking in her window late Friday night, the first night you visited me in the cottage. I, er, don't suppose—"

"I don't peer into bedroom windows, either," he said crossly. He still had his honor, for whatever it was worth now.

The memory flashed through his mind of standing beside Bailey's bed, watching her sleep. No need to mention that. The point was, he hadn't been lurking outside the inn, looking into windows.

"I didn't think you would. I just had to ask."

He nodded curtly.

Bailey laughed softly. "I've offended you. You've gotten all stiff and sulky again."

His eyebrows drew downward. "I don't sulk."

"I suppose you consider brooding manly," she said. "But it's still sulking."

He felt the corners of his mouth twitch in a reluctant smile. "Anna used to accuse me of the same thing."

"That doesn't surprise me. Were you and Anna close, before she married my brother?"

"Yes," he said, his smile fading. "We were very close."

"You must have missed her this past year."

He thought of the lonely grayness. "You couldn't know how much."

"I have a brother, too," she reminded him. "I missed Dean terribly when he moved here. I do understand."

He only nodded, knowing she couldn't guess at what real loneliness felt like. What it was like to face an eternity of solitude. He hoped Bailey would never know that fate.

He wished he knew exactly what he had done to deserve it, himself.

"You make me crazy, Bran Cameron," Bailey said after a moment. There was a hint of amusement in her voice, but it didn't show in her eyes.

"Why?"

"I think you already know the answer to that."

He smiled faintly. "Yes. I suppose I do."

"You're not exactly an average sort of guy, you know."

"Not exactly," he agreed, his smile deepening.

"You're secretive."

"Yes."

"And obstinate."

"Very likely."

"Deliberately enigmatic."

"Perhaps."

"Why do you keep coming around if you're so reluctant for me to learn anything about you?" she asked bluntly.

"Maybe I'd like to help *you*, Bailey," he suggested.

She looked surprised. "Help me? But I'm fine."

"You're unhappy."

"Just temporarily bummed," she said with a shrug.

He frowned. "Bummed?"

"Discouraged. I'll get over it."

"So there's no need for me to keep coming around, as you put it?"

She bit her lip. "I hope you don't stop."

"Why?"

"Because—" Her hand fluttered, as though in search of an answer. "Because I want to be with you," she answered finally.

Ian knew he was on dangerous ground, but he couldn't seem to back away. "Even though I make you crazy?"

"Maybe because you make me crazy," she whispered, looking at him with eyes that glowed in the soft, intimate lighting.

"You make me crazy, too, Bailey Gates," he murmured.

She leaned a little closer, as though to better hear his lowered voice. "Do I?"

He nodded, his gaze falling to her moistened, slightly parted lips. "You make me want—"

"What?" she whispered, her mouth only an inch from his now.

A groan pushed its way from somewhere inside him. "Things I can't have," he said roughly.

A moment later, he was on his feet, standing several feet away from where she sat blinking at his sudden movement. "Go inside, Bailey, and lock your doors. You'll catch cold out here in the night air."

"Bran—"

Just once, he thought, he'd like to hear his real name on her lips. "Good night, Bailey."

"But—"

He turned and walked rapidly away, into the darkness, into the rain he couldn't feel. He disappeared quickly into the shadows, before she could notice that his hair and clothing were still completely dry.

The weather had no effect on a ghost.

Bailey, on the other hand, was tearing him apart.

BAILEY SAT on her bed, her feet drawn up in front of her, and listened to the rain splashing against the bedroom window. Usually she enjoyed the peaceful sound of rain in the night. This particular night, it only seemed to emphasize how very much alone she was.

Maybe she should have taken a room in the inn. Aunt Mae would be close by, then, as well as the staff and guests. She would be surrounded by people.

But she would still be alone.

There was no one she could talk to about this, no one who would truly understand what a mess her life had become. No job, no home of her own except a small apartment in Chicago that held no pleasure for her now, no plans for her future. And now, to top everything off, she was falling hard for a man who seemed to have more secrets and more emotional barriers than anyone she'd ever made the mistake of getting involved with.

It was ridiculous for her to feel this way about Bran, she told herself, trying to be sensible and logical. She hardly knew him. She'd been with him—what? Three times? Four?

She wished he were with her now.

He was the most frustrating man she'd ever met. Though he somehow managed to get her to tell him things she didn't tell anyone else, he steadfastly refused to tell her anything at all about himself. She knew something had come between him and Anna, but he wouldn't discuss it. He was unemployed, and he'd made it clear that he wasn't looking for a relationship.

You make me want things I can't have, he'd said just before he'd moved away from her as though she'd explode in his face if he didn't.

She'd wanted him to kiss her so badly she'd ached.

She buried her face in the crook of her arms and groaned. *Oh, Bailey, you really are a fool,* she thought in despair. Something told her Bran could hurt her worse than she'd ever been hurt before.

She was just as certain that the hurt was already inevitable.

THE WATCHER WAS WET. He was cold. And he was furious.

She was inside, warm and dry and surrounded by people who seemed to be going out of their way to make her happy. She didn't deserve that after what she'd done to him.

He opened one of the little packages of white powder he had stored so carefully in his backpack. He needed something to warm him, to keep him going for another night. Something to help him think, help him plan.

He needed a plan if he was to have his revenge.

She hadn't taken him seriously, and now she had to pay. Soon. If innocent bystanders happened to get in the way, they would pay with her.

Nothing mattered to him now. Nothing but the bittersweet vision of vengeance.

ON MONDAY EVENING, Bailey, Mae, Cara and Casey loaded into Dean's car for the short ride to the Destiny Elementary School. The annual Fall Festival was to be held that night, and Casey was to sing with her fifth-grade class. She seemed delighted that Bailey and Mae wanted to attend. For the first time, Bailey saw the child so excited she was almost bouncing with energy.

"I hope I don't mess up," she fretted as Bailey pulled into the already-crowded parking lot of the school.

"You won't mess up," Cara assured her daughter patiently. "You've been practicing for weeks. You know these songs, honey."

"What if I have to sneeze or something right in the middle?"

Mae chuckled and patted the girl's cheek. "Then you just go right ahead and sneeze, sweetie. And do it with panache."

"What's pan—pan—"

"Panache," Mae repeated. "Flair. Style. Cool, as you kids would say."

"How can a sneeze be cool?" Casey asked, baffled.

Mae grinned. "Darling, cool is definitely in the eye of the beholder."

"You're confusing her, Aunt Mae," Bailey said, turning off the engine. "You'll do fine, Casey. I have full faith in you."

"Thanks, Bailey."

Cara looked even more nervous than her daughter as she gave her a final inspection before sending her backstage. Bailey thought the little girl looked adorable in her frilly pink dress, a matching pink bow restraining her white-blond curls. That now-familiar wistfulness gripped her as she watched Cara lean over to kiss her daughter's cheek for luck.

Bailey wanted very much to believe that someday she'd be attending a school program with her own child.

They were just taking their seats in the noisy auditorium, when Mark appeared beside them. "Mind if I join you?" he asked cheerfully.

Bailey and Mae promptly moved down, leaving an empty seat next to Cara. Mark took immediate advantage of the opening. Cara gave Mae and Bailey a look of reproach, but accepted Mark's presence with resignation.

Bailey hid a smile, noting Mark's smug expression as he settled more comfortably into the hard wooden seat. She noticed that he "accidentally" brushed Cara's arm a few times. Cara must have noticed, too, judging from the blush that stained her cheeks.

Looking more closely than she should have, Bailey decided that Cara didn't appear to be repulsed by Mark's touch. She believed Cara had deeper feelings for Mark than she allowed herself to show. If not, surely Cara would have been more resolute about putting an end to his tenacious pursuit.

Bailey was highly amused by the school program. It was hardly a flawless production, but it was sweet and sincere. The children were adorable—even the ones who squirmed and scratched during their performances. She had a much better time than she'd expected. And she only thought about Bran once every ten minutes or so during the evening.

Knowing how nervous Casey had been, Bailey held her breath all the way through the child's two songs, particularly when Casey stepped forward for her brief solo. She noticed that Cara, Mark and Mae also tensed, all of them wanting Casey to feel good about her performance later. They needn't have worried. Casey came through like a pro, singing with a confidence Bailey wasn't sure she could have managed had she been the one up there facing an enthusiastic audience.

Bailey and Mae applauded loudly at the end of the number. Cara slackened in relief, murmuring, "Thank heaven she didn't sneeze."

Mark grabbed the excuse to give Cara an exuberant, one-armed hug—strictly out of congratulations on her talented daughter, he assured her when Cara gulped a remonstration.

Bailey studied Mark out of the corner of her eye, wondering if he'd taken her advice seriously. Maybe he'd decided it was time to be a bit bolder with Cara. To make it just a little harder for her to politely elude him.

Casey's face lit up when she saw him waiting with the others after the program. "Hi, Mark!" she said. "Are you going to put my picture in your newspaper?"

"You bet," he assured her. "Maybe on the front page."

"No!" Cara protested quickly, a quick flare of panic in her eyes.

She made a visible attempt to collect herself. "I mean," she said more quietly, "this really isn't front-page news, sweetheart. Maybe just a little photo somewhere inside the paper would be better."

Mark looked searchingly at Cara, but he only nodded and squeezed Casey's little hand reassuringly. "It will be in there somewhere," he promised. "And now, how about we all go out for ice cream to celebrate your success? My treat."

Mae smiled, after giving Cara a quick, questioning look. "Thank you, Mark, but Elva made Casey's favorite banana-split cake for us to eat at our own private postperformance party. Elva worked hard on the dessert. She would be disappointed if we didn't eat it."

Cara surprised everyone by turning to Mark and saying, "Why don't you join us?"

He looked momentarily stunned, but recovered quickly. "Uh, yeah, sure. That would be great."

"I'm sure Casey wants you there," Cara added quickly.

Cara was distancing herself from the invitation, Bailey thought. But at least this time she had taken a step toward Mark instead of two steps away. That seemed a good sign.

Bailey gave him a quick thumbs-up when no one else was looking. He grinned and made a surreptitious gesture of wiping his forehead.

Fifteen minutes later, they were on their way, Bailey driving Mae, Cara and Casey in Dean's car, Mark following in his own.

"This is going to be fun," Casey said enthusiastically. "Our own private party with banana-split cake and soda. Thanks for asking Mark, Mommy. He'll like Elva's cake."

"Mark likes anything Elva cooks," Cara replied. "I just didn't want to be rude by not inviting him after he'd asked us out for ice cream."

"Well, I'm still glad he's coming," Casey said. "I like Mark. I think you should go out with him, Mommy."

Cara looked quickly at Mae and Bailey, who sat quietly in the front seat, not even pretending they weren't listening to every word. "Casey," she protested. "What makes you say that?"

Casey smiled archly. "I know he's been asking. I think you should go. Mark's cool. Cute, too. All the girls at school think so."

"They do, do they?"

"Yeah. Betty Anne Mayberry wants him to go out with *her* mom, 'cause her mom's divorced, but I told Betty Anne that Mark likes you."

"Casey!"

"Well, he does," Casey insisted.

"We'll talk about this later," she muttered.

"Don't stop talking about it on our account," Mae said brightly. "Bailey and I think you should go out with him, too, don't we, Bailey?"

Bailey laughed. "Now you're going to have Cara mad at all of us, Aunt Mae. Leave the poor woman alone. She'll make up her own mind."

"Thank you, Bailey," Cara said, sounding relieved.

"No problem. I'm convinced that you're smart enough to see that Mark's a fabulous guy who would happily cut off his arm if you asked him to. You don't need *us* to tell you that you'd be crazy not to give a guy like that a chance."

Cara covered her face with her hands. "Oh, thanks a lot."

Bailey grinned.

A massive pickup truck suddenly appeared out of no-where, speeding down the narrow country road directly in Bailey's path. Almost blinded by the high beams of the oncoming vehicle's headlights, Bailey swerved to the right and slammed her hand down on her horn, expect-ing the other driver to move quickly back to his own side of the road.

She was horrified when the truck swerved in the same direction she did, heading straight for Dean's car.

"He's going to hit us!" she screamed, dragging at the steering wheel with both hands, desperately searching the dark road for a safe refuge. "I can't—"

The truck broadsided them with a screech of tires and grinding crash of metal. Jarred by the impact, Bailey struggled for control, but the outcome was inevitable. Dean's compact car left the road and plunged down a wooded embankment, and there was nothing its occu-pants could do but brace themselves and pray.

CHAOS REIGNED at the usually quiet country roadside. Blue lights blazed from Destiny's two police vehicles, red lights spun on the ambulance and amber lights flashed atop the wrecker that was slowly dragging Dean's bat-tered car up the furrowed embankment.

There seemed to be uniforms everywhere. Bailey held a hand to her bleeding forehead and tried to make sense of the confusion.

Mercifully, no one had been seriously hurt in the crash. The car had come to rest in a ditch, one fender crumpled against a tree, the windshield and one side window shattered by branches, but there was no real damage to the inside of the vehicle. Everyone had been belted in, so the injuries were relatively minor.

Mae was shaken, but recovering with the help of an oxygen mask and the solicitous care of paramedics. Casey's arm had slammed against her door, and would require X rays. Cara was bruised and dazed, her eyes huge in her colorless face as she hovered over her frightened child.

Mark stood very close to Cara's side, his arm locked protectively around her waist. Mark had reached the car only moments after the impact.

Someone touched Bailey's arm as she was watching her aunt being helped into the ambulance. "Ma'am? We're taking everyone to be checked out at the hospital now. Let me help you into the ambulance."

"I'm fine," Bailey said, her voice tremulous. "Really." But she could feel the warmth of her own blood on her face, the throbbing of her shoulder where she'd slammed against the driver's door before being jerked back by her seat belt. Her left ankle felt hot and swollen; she hoped it was only sprained.

Despite her brave words, she was grateful for the support of the paramedic as she walked toward the ambulance in which Mae, Cara and Casey already sat.

"I'll follow you to the hospital," Mark said. "Chief Peavy's going to meet me there for a description of the truck that broadsided you. I hope they catch the son of a bitch soon. I want to personally smash the guy's face in."

Bailey bit her lip as she climbed into the ambulance, remembering that moment when she had swerved and the truck had so swiftly followed. Though she found it hard to believe, she couldn't shake the disturbing feeling that the crash had been no accident.

7

March 1, 1903

Ian ran away from home yesterday. He was missing for almost five hours before a neighbor found him. I was terrified that something had happened to him.

He simply can't accept that I am going to marry Gaylon. Ian keeps saying that he knows it's a mistake, that he is afraid that something terrible will happen if I marry him. I can't convince him that he is letting his imagination and his fear of change influence him. I don't believe he really intended to be gone for long—he would never have left Mary Anna—but he wanted to upset me. I suppose he thought I would now understand how deeply opposed to this marriage he is, and perhaps change my mind about going through with it.

I do understand. I still have my own doubts about the wisdom of my decision, but I can't let myself be influenced by a willful child's tantrums. Perhaps I have spoiled him. Maybe the others are right. Ian needs a father. I can no longer handle him alone. He is so stubborn, so convinced that he knows what is best for all of us, as young as he is. He has taken his role as the man of the household very seriously. He doesn't want to give it up. I wish he could understand that I want him to be a child while he still can. He will have to grow up all too quickly.

Mary Anna is the only one who can truly reach him. She was very angry with him for frightening us. She made him promise both me and her that he would never do such a thing again. He finally told me that if I am determined to marry Gaylon, he will try to accept it. He looked so unhappy that it broke my heart, but I'm sure everything will be fine now.

At least, I hope it will.

BAILEY MADE SURE her aunt was comfortably tucked in for the night before giving in to her own exhaustion that evening. Mae had recovered from the ordeal with amazing fortitude, and she resisted Bailey's efforts to hover over her.

"You go to bed and get some rest," Mae said flatly. "You were hurt worse than I was. In fact, I wish you'd stay in the inn tonight so we could keep a close eye on you."

Bailey shook her head, then regretted it when her battered temples pounded in protest. "I'm fine, Aunt Mae. I'll be more comfortable in the bed I've been sleeping in for the past two weeks. If you're sure you won't need me during the night, I'll go on out to the cottage."

"I won't need you," Mae said. "Elva insisted on spending the night when she heard what happened, and I'm sure she'll be in here half a dozen times checking on me. Cara will keep a close eye on Casey, but Elva will probably look in on them, too. You'll probably get more rest in the cottage. But you will call if you need anything, won't you?"

"I'll be fine. My ankle's only twisted and the cut on my head didn't even need stitches. No concussion, no broken bones, nothing at all for you to worry about tonight."

"It's a wonder no one was more seriously injured by that crazy drunk," Mae said with a sigh as she settled into the pillows.

Bailey nodded grimly, trying to hide her lingering misgivings about the so-called accident.

The police had failed to find the truck or its driver, though they were still looking. Everyone seemed to accept that the driver had been intoxicated, the crash merely a drunken miscalculation of speed and distance.

Bailey was having trouble accepting that explanation. She couldn't stop picturing those overbright lights heading steadily, certainly, in her direction.

She bent rather stiffly to kiss her aunt's pale cheek. "Good night, Aunt Mae. Sleep well."

"I'll certainly try. But it will be a while before I can forget the sound of that truck hitting us," Mae admitted.

Bailey shuddered. "Me, too."

Mark was waiting for Bailey outside Mae's bedroom. "I'll walk you to the cottage," he said. "Cara's putting Casey to bed."

"How's Casey doing?" Bailey asked, secretly grateful for Mark's supportive hand at her elbow.

"She's looking better. She made me promise I would sign her cast tomorrow."

"And Cara?"

Mark looked grim. "She hasn't said two words since the accident. She looks as if a strong wind could blow her right over. She wasn't hurt, physically, but she was badly frightened. And she won't let me close enough to help her."

Bailey thought of the way Cara had clung to Mark immediately after the accident. "Give her time, Mark," she advised. "She's still in shock. We all are, to an extent."

"Tell me about it. When I saw that truck hit you, and watched your car go off the road—"

His voice broke. It wasn't necessary for him to complete the sentence.

They walked out of the inn and down the path to the cottage in silence. They were almost to the door, when Mark spoke again. "Right after the accident, Cara said something that bothered me. It was almost as if she believed the crash was intentional."

Bailey stiffened. "Why would she think that?" she asked, hearing the odd note in her own voice.

"It was just something she said. Something like 'I knew this would happen.' Maybe she thinks this is connected in some way to whatever she's been here hiding from."

"You think Cara believes the driver of the truck was after *her?*"

"Yeah, from what she said, I think the possibility might have crossed her mind. Damn, I wish I had some idea of what happened to her."

"Whatever it is, she must be terrified."

"I don't know what to do, Bailey." He made the statement reluctantly, as though he wasn't accustomed to admitting defeat. "I don't know how to help her."

"Just be there for her. Let her know that you want to listen when she's ready to talk."

"Surely she knows that by now. I think I've made my feelings clear enough."

"Maybe she needs to keep hearing it until she's able to believe it. Don't give up on her, Mark."

"I won't," he said with a sigh. "I can't."

He took her key from her hand and unlocked the cottage door. "Do you need help with anything?" he asked.

Standing in the open doorway, she gingerly shook her head. "No, I'll be fine. Thank you for walking with me."

"Sure. I think I'll go back to the inn for a while. Maybe Elva will give me a cup of coffee. And maybe Cara will feel like talking after Casey's asleep."

"Maybe she will," Bailey said, though she didn't expect Cara to leave her child's side all night.

She stood in the open doorway until Mark had loped out of sight, with a final wave over his shoulder. She started to close the door, but froze when something moved at the very edge of her vision. Her fingers tightened convulsively on the doorknob, and she turned quickly, prepared to slam the door closed.

Bran stepped out of the shadows beside her porch. "Do you mind if I come in?" he asked quietly.

She sagged against the doorframe. "Someday you're going to give me a heart attack, skulking around like that," she muttered.

"I'm sorry. I didn't want to interrupt you and your friend."

Bailey was too weary and too troubled to dance around the truth tonight. "You mean you didn't want Mark to see you. Fine, Bran. If you want to keep playing your shadow games, go ahead. I won't reveal your secret identity."

He frowned. "I don't know what you're talking about."

"Neither do I," she admitted, pressing a hand to her pounding head. "I don't think I'd be very good company tonight, Bran. Maybe you'd better come back anoth—"

He moved forward so swiftly she blinked. "What happened to you?" he demanded, apparently just noticing the bandage on her forehead, as well as the sizable purplish lump it didn't quite conceal. "Are you all right?"

She sighed and stepped back from the door, letting him enter the cottage. She knew he wouldn't be leaving now until he'd heard everything. She closed the door and locked it, then limped toward the couch. "I was in a car accident."

Bran's hand moved toward her, as if he wanted to assist her, but he didn't touch her. "What happened? How badly are you injured?"

"A drunk driver in a half-ton pickup slammed into the side of the car I was driving and knocked me off the road. Aunt Mae and Cara and Casey were in the car with me. If we hadn't been belted in, or if the car had flipped, we'd have all been seriously injured. As it was, we were all bruised and battered, and Casey fractured her wrist, but she'll be fine."

"Your aunt is all right?"

Bailey was touched that he seemed so concerned about Mae. "She's okay. She's resting. Elva—the cook—is going to look in on her tonight."

"Who's going to look in on you?"

She leaned her head against the back of the couch and closed her eyes. "No one. I'm fine, Bran."

"You were limping."

"I twisted my ankle. Nothing serious, I promise."

"I'll stay with you tonight—for as long as I can."

"That isn't necessary, but thank you."

"I'm staying," he insisted.

She swallowed a groan of defeat. "Fine."

"Do you have anything to take for the pain?"

"I've already taken it. It's not too bad, just a pounding headache."

"You should be in bed."

She opened her eyes and looked at him, regretting the way she'd snapped at him. He looked so genuinely concerned for her, so anxious about her welfare.

She couldn't help softening. "I'm working up the strength to walk to the bedroom," she said with an attempt at a smile.

He didn't smile in return. "I wish there was something I could do to help you."

She made a weak effort to tease. "Okay, carry me."

His fists clenched at his sides. What might have been anguish crossed his face, so fleetingly she decided she must have imagined it.

"I'm afraid I can't do that," he said, no inflection at all in his voice.

Rather embarrassed, she gave a flat laugh and pushed herself off the couch. "Forget it. The medicine must be kicking in. I'm starting to feel light-headed."

"I'll wait in here while you dress. Call out when you're in bed, or—or if you need anything. Er, leave the door ajar so I can hear you if you call."

She nodded and limped toward the bedroom. She left the bedroom door open, as he'd ordered, and closed herself into the attached bathroom to change.

How did he do this to her? she wondered as she washed then tugged a soft T-shirt over her head. Here she was, battered and bruised, and yet she found herself hurting for *him*. Something about that look in his eyes had broken her heart.

She might be hurting physically, but Bran's pain was much deeper, much sharper. He was obviously suffering from something, and, as foolish as it might be, she cared enough about him to want to help him.

It seemed she hadn't learned from her mistakes, after all.

BRAN WAS WAITING by the bed when Bailey came out of the bathroom. She hadn't turned on the overhead light, so the glow from the lamp on the nightstand was the only illumination in the room. Bran's dark face was thrown into shadow, but she felt his eyes on her as she padded across the floor and climbed self-consciously into bed.

Ruefully, she thought that she certainly had no reason to be uneasy about being alone with Bran this way. Though he'd had ample opportunity, he'd never even touched her. He seemed to go out of his way to avoid doing so, in fact.

She wished she understood why.

Did he suspect that she was beginning to crave his touch with an intensity that shook her? When she was settled, Bran sat carefully on the side of the bed. "Are you in much pain?"

"No."

He smiled very faintly. "You're lying."

She smiled in return. "You're right."

"I wish there was something I could do to help you," he said again, his smile gone.

"Don't worry about it."

"You must have been terrified during the accident."

"I was furious," she said grimly. "The bastard that hit us was either drunk or—"

"Or?"

"Or deranged," she said quietly.

Bran tensed. "You think he did this on purpose?"

It sounded no more likely when Bran said it than it had sounded in her mind. "Probably not. I mean, why would he? But, well, it just seemed so deliberate. The police are looking for him for answers, but so far there's no trace."

Bran sat very still, his expression so hard that Bailey shivered. An almost palpable air of menace hovered around him. Mark had been angry, but not like this. Mark's anger was hot and fierce, normal under the circumstances.

Bran's temper was cold and dangerous.

"I'd like to spend some time with that driver when they find him," he said, his voice deadly soft.

Bailey tried to defuse his mood with a light tone. "Get in line. Mark's already expressed the desire to smash the jerk's face in."

Bran wasn't notably placated.

Bailey exhaled slowly. "What a day," she murmured.

"Get some rest. I'll let myself out in a while."

"Don't forget to lock the doors," she reminded him, smiling as she remembered the two times she'd left her door unlocked, allowing him to slip in and startle her.

Either he didn't catch the allusion, or he was too disturbed by what had happened to her to share her amusement. He only nodded. "I won't."

She nestled into the pillows. Bran stood. Bailey mused sleepily that he was lighter on his feet than any man she'd ever known. She rarely heard him move; she hadn't even felt the bed shift when he'd gotten up.

"G'night, Bran," she murmured, closing her eyes and allowing the pain medication to do its job.

"Good night, Bailey."

She liked the way he said her name, she thought as she drifted into a haze of exhaustion, discomfort and lingering shock. It sounded almost like an endearment. . . .

THE BLINDING LIGHTS were coming straight at her, murderous in their intent. Bailey stood paralyzed with fear in the middle of a deserted road, nothing between her and the metal monster barreling toward her. She tried to run, tried to scream, but she could do nothing but stare as those lights loomed larger and closer, the roar of the engine behind them almost deafening.

She realized suddenly that she wasn't alone. Little Casey crowded close against her, crying and trying ineffectively to hide behind Bailey as the vehicle bore down on them. Bailey threw her arms around the child, huddling over her, waiting for the inevitable impact—

"Bailey. Open your eyes, Bailey. Look at me."

The deep voice broke through the nightmare's cold grip. With a gasp and a shudder, Bailey opened her eyes.

Bran leaned over her, his expression grim. "Can you see me?" he asked.

Though she didn't quite understand why he'd phrased it that way, she nodded, and moistened her dry lips with the tip of her tongue. "I was dreaming," she said. "A nightmare."

He seemed to relax marginally. "I know. Are you all right?"

"Yes, I—" She cleared her husky voice. "I'm fine. What time is it?"

"Late," he replied without glancing at a clock.

She was shivering now. "Is it cold in here to you?"

"No."

She pulled the covers to her chin. "I'm cold."

"It's probably a reaction from your bad dream."

"Probably," she agreed with a sigh. "Have you gotten any sleep?"

"No."

"You should get some rest. It really isn't necessary for you to watch me all night."

"I'm not tired. And I told you that I intend to stay for as long as I can."

He'd said that before. "Is there something you have to do?"

"Yes. Later. For now, I'm here, if you want to talk. Or would you like to try to go back to sleep?"

She swallowed. "I'm not sure I can go back to sleep yet. The dream is still too fresh."

He sat on the bed, again so carefully that she hardly felt him. "Would you like to talk?"

"Mmm. Tell me something about yourself."

He smiled. "Are you trying to take advantage of my sympathy?"

"Maybe. Is it working?"

"No. But I will tell you that I had nightmares sometimes when I was a boy. My mother used to talk to me afterward until I went back to sleep."

"What were your nightmares about?" she asked, intrigued by this rare glimpse into his mysterious past.

"Change."

She lifted an eyebrow. "Change?"

He nodded, still smiling faintly, though his eyes were serious. "I was a very conservative child. I didn't like my comfortable routines disturbed."

"I would have thought you'd be the adventurous type. Always taking chances and getting into mischief."

"No. That was Anna. I was the one who tried to keep her from taking chances and then rescued her when she did."

"Her protector," Bailey murmured.

He nodded. "I thought it was my responsibility to take care of her and my mother. To keep them safe."

"What about your father?"

"He died before—when I was very young," he amended.

"So you became the man of the family," Bailey concluded. Was that why Anna's marriage had come between them? she wondered. Had Bran been reluctant to give up his lifelong role as her champion? Had he felt supplanted in his sister's life by Dean? Somehow, she thought there was more to it than that.

"Yes. Has Anna told you nothing of our family?"

"Not a thing. I don't even know how she and Dean met."

"I see."

"Of course, I've only been with her a few times," Bailey admitted. "And I was only here a week before she and Dean left for their vacation."

"Anna isn't one to talk about herself much."

Bailey yawned as her muscles began to relax. "She isn't the only one," she murmured.

Watching her closely, Bran nodded. "A family trait."

"Tell me more about your childhood," Bailey urged, squirming into a more comfortable position on her pillows. "Was your mother able to stop your nightmares?"

"Not entirely. She remarried when I was quite young. After that, I learned to keep my fears to myself."

"You didn't want her to remarry?"

"No."

"Didn't you like your stepfather?"

"No."

"Was he mean to her? Or to you?"

"No, he wasn't mean. He was just . . . dim."

She couldn't help smiling a little. "Dim? Do you mean he wasn't very bright?"

"He smiled a lot and said very little. Mother thought it was because he was quiet and reserved. I always thought it was because he had nothing of particular interest to say."

"Did he love your mother?"

"He was very fond of her inheritance from my father," Bran muttered.

"That doesn't sound very promising. Was she happy with him?"

"She never complained to me, but I don't think she was particularly happy. She died when I was a teenager. She contracted pneumonia after a long illness and just slipped away. It was almost as if she didn't care to live any longer."

"I'm sorry," Bailey whispered, hearing the echoes of pain in Bran's voice. "That must have been awful for you."

He nodded. "The next few years weren't particularly pleasant ones, either. I didn't get along with my stepfather, I couldn't get my hands on the—on my inheritance from my parents because of the terms of my mother's will. I was so angry, I ended up driving away most of my friends. If it hadn't been for Anna . . . but then I couldn't even protect her when it mattered most." He was looking away, his expression distant, his voice muted—almost as though he were speaking to himself.

"What do you mean you couldn't protect her?" Bailey asked carefully. "Did something bad happen to Anna?"

Bran seemed to rouse himself.

His frown told her that he'd said more than he'd intended. More than he wanted to reveal.

"Never mind that," he said. "The reason I told you these things is because I don't want you to make the same mistakes I did. Life is too short to waste with useless regrets. Don't dwell on the unpleasant things that have happened to you, or continue to blame yourself for the failings of others. Put it behind you and start making a new life for yourself. You have so much to offer, and you deserve so much in return. I want you to be happy, Bailey."

She looked at him in surprise. He'd spoken so forcefully, so intensely. It was probably the most he'd ever said to her at one time.

It had sounded suspiciously like a farewell speech.

"Bran?" she asked uncertainly. "Why are you saying this now? You aren't going away, are you? You'll stay until Anna returns, won't you?"

"I have to go now," he said, his expression reluctant. "I'm sorry I can't stay with you longer tonight. Will you be all right? Should you call someone?"

"I'll be fine," she said impatiently, rising to one elbow. "Where are you going? When will you come back?"

"I don't know," he said. "I can't explain now, but I'll try to come back as soon as I can to make sure you're all right. If I can't, remember what I said, will you?"

"Yes, but—"

He was already moving away from the bed. She reached out to him, her fingers clutching empty air as he stepped just out of reach. "Bran, wait."

"I'm sorry, Bailey." He looked harried now, as though he must hurry. "I have to go."

Her hand fell. Swallowing hard, she nodded stiffly against the pillow. "I won't keep you, then."

He hesitated, glancing from the open bedroom doorway and then back to her. "Take care of yourself."

"I will." She had no other choice.

Still he lingered, his gaze locked on her battered face. "I don't like leaving you like this."

She started to tell him she understood. She kept silent because she *didn't* understand. She had no idea what was suddenly calling him away. Why he couldn't tell her when he would return—if at all.

He took a step closer to the bed and leaned over her. "I'm sorry," he murmured. "About everything."

His face was so close to hers that she should have felt the warmth of his breath on her skin. He seemed to be holding it. Her own breath was lodged behind a massive lump in her throat.

He moved closer, paused, then brushed his lips across her bruised forehead, so lightly she felt little more than a shivery tingle where he touched her.

She closed her eyes as her pulse raced in response to the brief caress. When she opened them again, he was gone.

She looked toward the open doorway through which he must have silently made his escape. The cottage was dark beyond that door, quiet. Empty.

"Good night, Bran," she murmured.

She hoped with all her heart that it wasn't goodbye.

IAN CURSED the grayness. Cursed the silence. Cursed himself for leaving Bailey confused and vulnerable, hurting from her injuries, still shaken from the aftermath of her nightmare.

Would she awaken again, whimpering and fearful, with no one there to hear her? No one to reassure her?

In her own way, she was as much alone as he was. He ached at the memory of her lying so pale and so uncharacteristically subdued against the pillows. Someone should be with her. Someone to comfort her. Care for her. Guard her.

Someone who could have carried her to her bed and tenderly tucked her in.

His fists clenched at the thought of anyone other than himself doing those things for her. Yet how could he deny her what he could never offer?

It would probably be better for both of them if he never saw her again. If they'd never met at all.

He'd only wanted to help her, to be a friend when she needed one, but it had grown beyond that. Something serious was building between them. Something that had the potential to be very painful for both of them.

What would happen if she learned the truth about him? Would she hate him? Pity him? Fear him?

He didn't want to face any of those possibilities.

He reminded himself that it had worked out for Anna. Maybe . . . maybe the same thing could happen for him and Bailey.

But, no. He had nothing to offer her. No job, no future, no security, no home. The inn belonged to Dean and Anna now.

He had no knowledge of her world, her society, her history, the technology she so casually took for granted—even her words were foreign to him at times. He would be useless to her, no better than those men in her past—indigent, uncertain, dependent on her to help him find his way.

The imagery made him cringe.

He knew he should stay away from her. But he was consumed with the need to know that she was all right. To see her. To hear her voice. To be close to her . . . even if he couldn't touch her. Could never have her.

Suddenly overcome with rage and frustration, he threw back his head and let out an anguished shout.

There was no sound in the grayness. Only the dim echoes of pain and hopelessness reverberating through his mind.

8

November 11, 1903

Gaylon and I returned from our honeymoon trip to New Orleans yesterday. Though I was weary from the long train ride, I tried to enjoy the welcome-home party the staff had waiting for us. It went very well. Ian and Mary Anna were on their best behavior, and young Charles participated a bit more than he usually does. I smiled until my face ached.

To an outsider, we would have appeared to be a very happy family, indeed. I, however, was much too aware of how mistaken that impression would have been.

I know how unhappy my children really are about the marriage, though to their credit, they are trying to support me. I sense that Charles isn't at all excited about leaving the farm where he grew up to move into the inn with his new family. As for me, I knew on my wedding night that I had made a sad mistake.

Gaylon tried to make it pleasant for me. He was very patient and gentle. But though I will try to be a good wife to him, I cannot feign enthusiasm for an act that I find holds little appeal for me now. When

I allow myself to remember the way it was with James, I become almost physically ill at the thought of letting Gaylon touch me that way again. There is no joy for me in lovemaking now, only regrettable comparisons, though I will do my best to hide my true feelings.

Poor Gaylon. He deserves better. But I have nothing more to give.

I should have known better. I should have realized that a marriage without love is wrong. I should have listened to my children, instead of all those well-intentioned people who do not truly know me. But it's done now. And for all our sakes, I will make it work. I must lock the bittersweet memories away and concentrate on my children's future.

BAILEY WAS NOT overly impressed by the Destiny police force, not even when the chief himself arrived at the inn the next afternoon to report the latest development in the investigation.

"Just thought I'd let you people know that we've found the truck that hit you," the mousy-looking man in the wrinkled brown uniform reported officiously. "It was stolen from a motel over on the other side of town. Whoever was driving the vehicle when it hit you was long gone. He abandoned the truck in the parking lot of the Piggly Wiggly."

Bailey, Mae, Cara and Mark sat in the lobby of the inn, paying close attention as Chief Roy Peavy made his announcement. They exchanged a look of shared dissatisfaction when he finished.

"That's it?" Bailey asked, the first to speak up. "That's all you have?"

Peavy nodded stiffly, his gray eyebrows beetled over his cool brown eyes. "That's all we have at this point. We're still looking for clues and interviewing potential witnesses. We expect the perpetrator to be apprehended. But it takes time to complete an official investigation."

He sounded as though he was quoting from an official police-spokesperson's phrase book, Bailey thought in exasperation. "What time was the truck reported stolen?" she asked.

"Fifteen minutes before you say the accident happened. The owner was . . . entertaining a ladyfriend in a motel room when the truck was taken."

"He left the keys in it?" Mae asked.

Peavy shook his head. "It was hot-wired."

"No one saw anything?" Mark asked with a frown. "It's not as if it were stolen in the middle of the night. It couldn't have been much past nine o'clock."

"As I said," Peavy replied, "we are interviewing potential witnesses. Unfortunately, the staff and clientele of this particular motel don't tend to be overly cooperative with the police. We suspect that the truck was stolen by some joyriding teenagers, probably drunk or high on something. When they hit you, they most likely panicked, abandoned the truck as soon as they could and hightailed it out of there."

"What about the scene of the wreck?" Bailey asked. "Are you looking for clues there, as well?"

Peavy looked a bit confused. "We're sure we have the truck that hit you. The one we found matches the description you gave us, and the left side sustained heavy damage. We'll test the paint scrapings against your car, but I'm sure we'll find that it's the right vehicle."

"What about skid patterns, or whatever you call them? Has anyone studied them?" Bailey asked. "Can you tell if the other driver tried to avoid us? Was there any indication that he applied his brakes? Did his driving appear to be erratic, or was it controlled?"

Peavy was looking at her now with a suspicious frown. "You make it sound like you're asking if there's any evidence that he ran into you on purpose."

Cara gasped, then looked quickly down at her clenched hands. Sitting beside her on the small sofa, Mark slid an arm around her shoulders. She didn't relax into the comforting embrace, but she didn't pull away, either, Bailey noted.

"You have reason to think someone's out to hurt you, Ms. Gates?" Peavy demanded.

"I was just asking about the details of your investigation."

"You aren't thinking the Peavy family has anything to do with this, are you? Because if you are—"

"Chief Peavy, I have no reason to accuse your family of anything," Bailey assured him flatly. "Why would I?"

He searched her face for a moment, looking torn between answering her question and ignoring it. Bailey knew what was agitating him, of course. She'd been told that Peavys' overbearing aunt, Margaret Peavy Vandover, had hired someone to intimidate Dean into keeping quiet about her late father's involvement in the murders of the Cameron twins.

Dean had been brutally attacked and injured. It was fortunate that he hadn't been killed. Due to Margaret's age and precarious emotional state, he hadn't pressed charges, but he'd made it clear that he would tolerate no further harassment from the Peavy family. They hadn't bothered him since.

"My family had nothing to do with this," Peavy said after a moment. "We don't like what your brother did to our family's reputation, and I can't say any of us like him all that much—"

Peavy gave Mark a glance that included him in his family's list of least favorite people.

"But," he added firmly, "my generation is respectable and law-abiding. I've sworn to serve and protect the citizens of this area, Ms. Gates. If anyone out there is trying to harm you, or any member of your family, you can bet I'll do my job to the best of my ability."

He had definitely memorized the cop phrase book, Bailey decided. But she couldn't doubt the man's sullen sincerity.

She met his eyes squarely. "I believe that you and your family mean us no harm, Chief Peavy. And I can assure you that I can think of no one who would have deliberately staged that accident last night. If I had any knowledge of who was behind it or why, I would have already told you. I just wanted to make sure that every possibility is being considered in your investigation."

He nodded, looking only partially mollified. "We'll be thorough, Ms. Gates. We'll catch the guy."

"Whew," Mark said a few minutes later, when the prickly officer had made his exit. "You and your brother are determined to stay off the Peavy family's Christmas-card list, aren't you?"

Mae didn't smile. She was looking at Bailey in concern. "Bailey, why did you ask Chief Peavy those questions? You don't really think the accident was intentional, do you? Is there any chance this has anything to do with that man in Chicago?"

"Larry?" He'd crossed her mind a few times, but she'd come to the conclusion that she was just being paranoid. She wrinkled her nose and shook her head. "He was a real nuisance to me there, but he wouldn't go to the trouble of following me all the way here. I made it clear to him before I left that I wanted him to leave me alone. I'm sure he got the message. And besides, he has a business to run."

Bailey turned her attention to Cara. The housekeeper was still pale, sitting stiffly beside Mark, her eyes locked on her hands.

Bailey didn't want to badger Cara about her past, but if any of them were in danger because of it, she thought they had a right to know. She couldn't forget that moment when those lights had borne down on them, so steadily, so inexorably.

"Cara?" she asked gently. "What about you? Can you think of anyone who wants to harm you? Someone ruthless enough to have caused that accident last evening?"

What little color was left in Cara's face drained. "Why do you ask that?" she asked hoarsely. "Why would you think this had anything to do with me?"

"Cara, as far as I know, it really was just a truckload of stoned teenagers," Bailey answered frankly. "But until we know for sure, I think we should look at all the possibilities, don't you?"

Cara bit her lip, her gaze locked with Bailey's. She looked scared, uncertain, on the verge of tears. She drew a deep breath, and Bailey held hers, hopeful that Cara was finally going to level with them.

And then Mark inadvertently ruined the moment. "We want to help you, Cara," he said, leaning closer to her. "Tell us what happened to you before you came here."

It was as though she suddenly slammed a mental door between her and the rest of them.

She rose abruptly, putting physical, as well as emotional, distance between herself and Mark. "I'd better go check on Casey," she said. "It's time for her medication."

"Cara, please," Mark said, his hand rising as though to reach for her. "Talk to us."

Cara raked him with eyes so cold that Bailey shivered in reaction. She could only imagine how Mark must have felt, being on the receiving end of that stare.

"If you're angling for a juicy story for your newspaper, I'm afraid you'll have to look elsewhere," Cara said, her tone uncharacteristically hard. "I really have nothing to say to the press."

Bailey was stunned by the unfairness of the attack. Mae murmured an incoherent protest.

Mark looked devastated. His hand fell heavily to his side.

"I wasn't asking as a reporter," he said, his voice husky. "Surely you know me well enough to trust me that much."

"I don't trust anyone who makes a living exposing other people's secrets," she muttered.

His face hardened. "If I was only interested in exposing secrets, I'd have plenty to tell about this place," he snapped. "Dean and Anna trust me. What have I done to make you think so badly of me?"

Bailey wondered what he meant. Mae looked troubled by his words. Cara's only reaction seemed to be weary regret.

"I'm sorry," she said, apparently speaking to all of them. "I—I really must go see about Casey now."

She all but bolted from the lobby, leaving a taut silence in her wake.

"Well," Mark said after a moment, his green eyes bleak. "I guess she made that clear enough."

Bailey ached in sympathy for him. "She's frightened, Mark. I don't know why, but she's terrified of something. And obviously, she's had a bad experience with the press."

"I'm not 'the press,' damn it," he growled. "I'm the guy who was stupid enough to fall in love with her."

He rubbed his forehead with a visibly unsteady hand. "I need to get out of here for a while. You'll call if you need me, won't you?"

"Of course we will." Mae rose as Mark did. She tugged at his hand, pulling him downward so that she could kiss his cheek.

"Cara isn't a deliberately cruel woman," she murmured reassuringly. "She's probably already very sorry that she spoke the way she did. I'm sure if you give her time . . ."

"Thanks for the encouragement, Mae, but I just don't know how much more time I can give her," Mark muttered. "A man can only take so much rejection."

Mae sighed. "I understand."

"Maybe I could talk to her for you," Bailey offered.

Mark patted her cheek. "I know you mean well, but stay out of it, Bailey. This is between Cara and me. One way or another, it's going to have to be up to us to settle it."

She nodded. "You're right, of course."

She wanted very badly to ask what he'd meant when he'd referred to the secrets he could expose about the inn and its inhabitants, and why he'd made it sound so significant that Dean and Anna trusted him. But she knew this wasn't the right time.

He left without saying anything more.

"Poor Mark," Mae said with a sigh. "And poor Cara. I hate to see them both suffering so."

Bailey touched a hand to the sore lump on her forehead, and felt a pounding headache starting to develop behind it. "It seems like everyone around here has secrets," she muttered. "Cara, Mark, Dean, Anna, Bran. Even you. I feel like an outsider."

"Oh, sweetheart, I'm sorry you feel that way," Mae said, turning immediately to her niece. "I'm sure none of us are deliberately trying to exclude you. As for me, I don't have any dark secrets I'm keeping from you. Only—only suspicions that aren't really mine to share."

Bailey wished she'd kept quiet. Now Mae was upset, worried that she'd somehow hurt her beloved niece's feelings. "I know, Aunt Mae. I'm sorry. I guess we're all still perturbed about last night."

"Yes," Mae agreed, continuing to look troubled. "It has been a tense day."

"I think I'll go rest for a while. Why don't you do the same?"

"I believe I will. Thank goodness, we only have four rooms occupied right now. Elva and Millie can handle the inn until we're back to normal. I hope Dean and Anna are having a lovely time, but I will certainly be glad to turn everything over to them again when they return."

"I haven't been helping very much, have I? Is there anything I can do this afternoon? Paperwork, or errands, or—well, anything?"

Mae smiled and shook her head. "Thank you, dear, but everything is under control for now. I promise I'll let you know if there's anything you can do."

"I'll hold you to that."

Bailey was on her way out, when her aunt stopped her. "Bailey?"

"Yes, Aunt Mae?"

"Who is Bran?"

Bailey froze. Had she really said his name aloud?

She swallowed, thinking how unfair she'd been to complain of the others' secrets when she was keeping a rather sizable one of her own. "I'll—I'll tell you later, okay, Aunt Mae?"

Her aunt cocked her head in curiosity, but didn't press. "Whenever you're ready."

Bailey swallowed a groan. And to think she'd come to Arkansas to escape from her problems!

Had she known that within two weeks of her arrival she would be falling in love with a man who was probably going to break her heart, that she would barely escape a tragic car accident and would get caught in the middle of a stormy romance between her brother's friends, she probably would have stayed in Chicago.

SHE HADN'T BEEN KILLED. Not even seriously injured, from what he could tell.

He doubled his fist and slammed it against his thigh. He thought he'd been so clever. Thought it would have looked like an unsolved hit-and-run accident, probably blamed on kids. His name would never have come up. No one around this hick town had ever heard of him. No one would have guessed that only one person out of the carful of females had been targeted for retaliation.

It looked as if he was going to have to take care of this the old-fashioned way, he thought as he ripped open a packet of powder with his teeth. Close up and in person.

There'd be more satisfaction that way, anyway.

It no longer mattered to him if he was caught. What more did he have to lose?

She was going to pay for the humiliation she'd caused him.

BRAN WAS WAITING outside the cottage when Bailey arrived.

She tried to hide the rush of sheer relief she felt when she saw him, though she suspected she wasn't overly successful. "I wasn't sure you would come today."

His own expression was shuttered, though his eyes searched her face with an intensity that made her tremble. "I wasn't sure I could. But I very much wanted the chance to make sure you're all right."

"As you can see, I'm fine." Forcing her hand to hold steady, she stuck her key in the lock. "Come in. I'll make coffee or something."

"I can't stay."

She tensed at the heaviness of his voice, sensing that he was turning down more than coffee.

"Can't? Or won't?" she asked, staring fixedly at the doorknob to avoid his eyes.

"Does it matter?"

"Yes," she whispered. The doorknob blurred through the film of tears in her eyes. "Yes, Bran. It matters."

"Bailey—"

She shoved open the door. "Never mind. If you want to go, I won't detain you."

"Bailey, you don't understand."

"No, I *don't* understand!" she snapped as she stepped into the cottage and spun to face him. "How can I? You won't tell me anything. No one around here will tell me anything, damn it!"

He stepped inside, leaving the door open behind him. "I didn't want to hurt you," he said, watching her with tormented eyes. "I only wanted to help."

She drew a deep breath, trying to regain her composure, clinging to what little pride she had left. "I'm sorry. I don't mean to embarrass you, or make you uncomfortable."

His mouth twisted. "You have no idea what it is you do to me. That's why I thought it would be best if I stay away."

She froze, searched his face, then took a step closer to him, wondering if she imagined the undercurrents of desire in his voice. "Bran?"

"I'm not leaving because I don't want you, Bailey," he said, his voice so low she barely heard him. "I'm leaving because I want you so badly it's tearing me apart."

She felt her eyes widen, her heart begin to thud in a heavy, nervous rhythm. She twisted her hands in front of her, eager, uncertain, bewildered. "You—you do?"

"I have from the first time I saw you. I knew even then that I couldn't stay with you, didn't have the right to even talk to you. But after you saw me that day in the gazebo, I—I couldn't stay away."

"I didn't want you to stay away," she said quietly.

"I didn't expect—didn't think you would—"

"Fall for you?" Bailey asked simply. "Well, I have."

He winced. "I'd forgotten that tendency of yours to speak your mind so frankly."

"I don't like dancing around the truth. It doesn't accomplish anything."

"Bailey, we can't do this," he said, visibly torn. "I can't be what you want. What you need."

She took some hope from the longing in his voice. She stepped closer to him, so close she almost touched him. She kept her hands at her sides, leaving that first move to him. "And how do you know what I want or what I need?" she challenged.

His hand rose, as though to touch her face. He held it poised an inch away from her cheek. "I know you don't need me."

"You're wrong."

His eyelashes flickered, the only indication of his emotions. "There are . . . things about me that you don't know."

"So tell me."

His hand still suspended in the air, he closed his eyes. His face convulsed in visible pain. "I was hoping I wouldn't have to."

Her throat tightened. She could almost feel the waves of unhappiness radiating from him, and she ached in sympathy.

She couldn't wait any longer for him to close the distance between them. She reached out to touch her fingertips to his face. "Oh, Bran, please talk to me. Tell me what it is that's hurting you so badly. Let me help."

His skin was cold beneath her fingers, almost icy. She wondered at that. Was this his reaction to extreme emotion? Was he ill? "Bran?"

His eyes opened, locked with hers. The heat in them belied the coolness of his skin. He started to speak.

She held her breath in anticipation.

"Bailey?" The woman's voice sounded from just beyond the open door, shattering the moment of intimacy.

Bailey dropped her hand and turned quickly toward the sound, aware that Bran had gone tense beside her. Elva Tippin stood framed in the doorway, a covered plate in her hands, a puzzled expression on her face. "Were you talking to someone?" she asked.

Bailey frowned, thinking the question strange. Obviously she'd been talking to Bran. She didn't bother to answer, but asked instead, "Do you need something, Elva?"

The woman walked through the doorway. "I brought you a snack. I made a chocolate-fudge cake for Casey and I took a piece up to your aunt. Thought I'd bring you a slice while I was at it."

"That was very thoughtful of you, Elva. Thank you," Bailey forced herself to say politely.

She wondered if she should introduce Bran, or if he would prefer to keep his identity private until his sister returned. She glanced at him in question, noting that his face was frozen, his mouth grim. Was he really that upset that someone else had finally seen him?

"How's your head? And your ankle?" Elva asked, setting the plate on the counter that separated the living room from the kitchenette.

"Better, thank you."

"If you need anything, you call me, okay? I don't like the thought of you being out here alone after that terrible accident last night. I told your aunt you should've stayed in the inn so I could keep an eye on you, but she said you're the independent type."

"She's right," Bailey admitted with a slight smile. "And besides," she added with a gesture toward Bran, "I'm not exactly alone."

Elva lifted a questioning eyebrow. "What do you mean?" she asked, looking straight at Bran. "Do you have company? Someone in the other room? I'd have brought two slices of cake if I'd known."

Bailey felt as though the world suddenly tilted. What in the world was going on? Elva was looking at Bran—looking *through* Bran, as though—

As though she didn't even see him.

"Bailey?" Elva asked in concern. "Honey, you've gone pale. Are you sure you aren't in pain? Maybe you'd better take one of those pills and lie down. I have to get ready for the dinner customers, but I can send Millie out to sit with you. Or better yet, come inside with me. You don't need to be out here by yourself when you're feeling so poorly."

By yourself.

Bailey stared helplessly at Bran, silently begging for an explanation.

"She can't see me," he said quietly. "She won't hear me, either."

Bailey swiveled her eyes toward the older woman. "You—you don't hear anything?"

Elva was beginning to look genuinely concerned. "Like what?"

Bailey couldn't answer.

"I'd better call the doctor," Elva said. "I think maybe you have a concussion, after all. Sit down, honey, and I'll—"

"No." Bailey held up a shaking hand. "No, Elva, really. I'm fine. I don't need a doctor."

"But—"

"Please," Bailey whispered. "I just need to be—to be alone for a few minutes, if you don't mind. I don't mean to worry you, and I appreciate your concern, but there are . . . things I need to do."

Elva looked torn between concern for Bailey and the need to go back to work. "You sure?"

"I'm sure. I'll be in later for dinner. If I need anything in the meantime, I only have to pick up the phone."

"Okay, then. Have it your way." Elva glanced furtively in Bran's direction, as though wondering what Bailey found so fascinating there. "Uh—enjoy your cake, Bailey."

"Thank you, Elva." Bailey walked her to the door, resisting an impulse to put a hand on the woman's arm to hurry her on her way. She closed the door behind Elva, and sagged bonelessly against it, needing just a moment to collect herself.

She drew a deep breath for courage, and then turned to demand some answers.

Only Bran wasn't there.

The room was empty.

Hauntingly empty.

"No!"

Bran threw out his hands, but his fingers closed around cold, barren mist. The change had been so fast this time, so jarringly abrupt that he'd had no chance to prepare himself, no time to say goodbye. One moment he'd been with Bailey, seeing the blank, hurt confusion in her eyes, the next moment he'd been snatched back to the place he despised so vehemently.

"No, damn it!" he shouted, his voice no more than a whisper in the gray emptiness surrounding him. "Not now. I can't leave her like this! I have to explain."

No one answered his impassioned plea.

No one was there to hear him.

Bran buried his face in his hands and gave in to despair.

9

February 14, 1906

My children, my babies, are ten years old. Ten years. It hardly seems possible.

I watched them tonight at dinner. They're healthy, thank God, and growing so quickly. I could see in their young faces the adults I believe they will become.

Mary Anna. My sweet, darling girl. Still as headstrong and impulsive as ever, but so loving. So thoughtful. She will be a good wife, a devoted mother. She radiates love. I can think of no more fitting birth date for her than St. Valentine's Day. I hope she will one day meet someone who will understand what a true and rare treasure he has found in her.

Ian. I am shaking my head even as I write his name. How can a child be so difficult, and yet so very special? There are times when I cannot imagine what is going on inside his head. He's changed so much since I married Gaylon. He is no longer the little boy he once was. He keeps his thoughts to himself now, for the most part, except with Mary Anna, who knows him better than any of us. He doesn't have many friends. I believe he intimidates the other children. He is so serious, so intense. So much an adult in a child's body.

He is a beautiful young man. He has thick, dark hair, and smoldering dark eyes, and his smile is devastating. I could never forget what my darling James looked like. I have only to look at Ian to call his father's image to mind perfectly.

Ian is like James in so many ways. When he gives his love, he gives it completely. Fiercely. He feels that way now about Mary Anna, and about me, and about our inn. I hope that someday he will share that devotion with a woman who will love him as passionately in return, a woman who can calm the storms of his turbulent soul, as James once told me I did for him.

James has been so prominent in my thoughts recently, perhaps because I know how proud he would have been of our children on their tenth birthday. Gaylon is jealous. He has finally realized, I think, that I will never love him the way I loved James.

He actually shouted at me the other evening, when we had a disagreement about the running of the inn. He accused me of living in the past, of being unfaithful to him in my thoughts and my dreams. In my heart. I told him quite frankly that I will continue to be a good wife to him, as I have tried very hard to be these past two and a half years, but that I will never forget my first husband, the father of my children. I didn't want to hurt him, but he should not have criticized me when I made no secret from the beginning that my love for James has never waned. Nor will it ever.

Mary Anna overheard our quarrel. I thought she was in bed, but she had gotten up for water. I regret deeply that she heard Gaylon's accusations. I tried to explain to her later that all married couples have their disagreements, but she still seemed troubled. She is fond of Gaylon, in her way, though Ian continues to treat him with the polite distance he maintains with guests of the inn and members of the staff.

I have given up hoping that Ian will ever accept Gaylon as a father. Gaylon, too, seems to have stopped trying. If, in fact, he ever really did. Sometimes I wonder if his pretty words of family were motivated more by his desire for the inn than his true feelings for me or my children. He shows favor to his own son, which is natural, I suppose, and he is kind to Mary Anna, but he does not reach out to Ian. At least he is never unkind to the children. He knows I would not tolerate it. And he is not a cruel man. Merely a thoughtless one, at times.

It grows late. I should go to bed. My husband will be wondering what is keeping me.

BAILEY SAT on the floor of the cottage, her back pressed to the door, her gaze fixed on the place where Bran had last stood. She didn't know how long she'd been sitting there—minutes? hours?—but she couldn't seem to move. *Elva hadn't seen or heard Bran.*

She kept replaying the times she'd spent with him. The odd things he'd said and done.

"There are many things about me that you would probably find very hard to believe."

"You make me want . . . things I can't have."

"I can't be what you want. What you need."

She thought of his almost obsessive avoidance of touching her. His sudden appearances and disappearances. The soundless way he moved.

He had never once knocked on her door, she realized dimly.

What *was* he?

A delusion? Had the series of misfortunes she'd suffered pushed her over the edge? Had she created a dark, handsome, brooding lover out of her wistful romantic fantasies?

He'd seemed so real.

An angel? He'd said several times that he wanted to help her. He'd listened to her problems, bolstered her battered ego, comforted her after her nightmare. And then she remembered his flashes of temper, his moodiness, the visible desire in his eyes when he'd leaned close and whispered that he wanted her.

She couldn't really picture Bran as an angel.

One word kept echoing through her mind, despite her efforts to ignore it. It was the one word she just wasn't ready to face.

But it simply wouldn't go away.

Ghost.

She groaned and leaned her head back against the hard wooden door.

Ghost. She'd never really thought about them, beyond the realms of fiction and fantasy. Had she been asked, she probably would have said she didn't truly believe in them.

She would have laughed if anyone had suggested she would fall in love with one.

She wasn't laughing now.

Still sitting on the floor, she buried her face in the crook of her arms and tried to make sense of a reality that had just taken a dramatic shift. Bran had stood right beside her, spoken to her, and Elva had neither seen nor heard him. Assuming that Bailey was still in her right mind—and she wouldn't want to bet her life savings on that at the moment—that meant Bran wasn't of her world. Which left her with two options—angel or ghost.

The latter seemed the inevitable deduction.

Okay, she thought as her heart raced in acceptance of the awesome truth. She had to be logical about this. As much as possible, anyway.

The only ghost stories she'd heard in connection with the inn had to do with the murdered Cameron twins. Could Bran possibly be the spirit of Ian Cameron? And if he was, did that mean—

Bailey lifted her head abruptly as several other realizations occurred to her almost simultaneously. Bran had claimed that Anna was his sister. No one knew exactly how Dean and Anna had met. Dean and Anna refused to discuss the legend, making it very clear that they wanted the stories to fade from public memory.

Anna's voice rang clearly in Bailey's thoughts, echoing words Bailey had overheard, but hadn't entirely understood.

"I can't bear to think that he might still be just drifting, all alone. I suppose I'm afraid to leave because I cling to the hope that he'll come back to me someday. Somehow. What if I'm not here when he tries to reach me?"

"No," Bailey murmured aloud. "Anna is alive. She's pregnant, for heaven's sake. She couldn't be—"

Was it possible—was there any way that Anna Cameron Gates was Mary Anna Cameron, murdered in 1921, miraculously brought back to life seventy-five years later?

Bailey pushed herself to her feet. She pressed a hand to the door when the room seemed to tilt for a moment. She was still half in shock.

She needed answers. Since Bran hadn't stayed around to provide them, she went looking for the one person who had always been there when Bailey needed help.

MAE WAS in the sitting room, her feet propped up, her needlework in her lap. She was still a bit pale from the ordeal of the night before, but was obviously well on the road to recovery.

She looked up with a smile when Bailey came into the room. "Hello, dear. Did you have a nice nap?" And then her smile faded. "What is it, darling? Is your head hurting? Have you taken one of your pills?"

Her head did ache, Bailey realized, but she brushed the observation aside. She had more important things to worry about now than a bump on her forehead.

She took a seat in the chair closest to her aunt's. She wanted to come right out and demand to know everything Mae knew, or even suspected, about the Cameron ghosts, but she had a feeling she wouldn't get very far with that tactic. Mae had proven very loyal to Dean and Anna, and very protective of their privacy, even with Bailey.

Bailey certainly couldn't fault her for that, but she needed to know the truth. And she wasn't ready to explain yet, even to Aunt Mae, why it had become so terribly important to her.

"My head is hurting a little," she admitted, deciding to start with a bid for sympathy. "I couldn't seem to relax."

"I'm sorry, dear. Should we call the doctor? Is there anything I can do?"

"I don't need a doctor," Bailey said, rather ashamed of herself. "I suppose I'm still just keyed up over everything."

"And no wonder," Mae said, clucking sympathetically. "It must have been terrible for you to have been driving when the accident happened. You must have been so frightened, and so concerned about your passengers."

"Yes," Bailey said with complete honesty. "It was a harrowing experience. I was so afraid I couldn't react quickly enough and you and Cara and Casey would suffer because of it."

"I'm very proud of you for the way you handled it, Bailey. It's probably because of your driving that no one was more seriously injured. We're all grateful to you."

Bailey flushed and squirmed in her seat. Now she really felt guilty. Nevertheless, she determinedly eased the conversation into the direction she wanted it to go.

"I was sitting out in the cottage, trying to take my mind off the wreck, and I started thinking about the history of the inn," she said, hoping her voice didn't sound as odd to her aunt as it did to her. "You kept copies of Mark's article, didn't you?"

"Why, yes. There are copies in Dean's office. Er, what made you think of them?"

"Just curiosity," Bailey replied, inwardly cringing at the lie. She just couldn't tell Aunt Mae everything. Not yet. Not until she knew exactly what was going on. She was terribly afraid she might start crying if she did—and if that happened, she wasn't at all sure she would be able to stop.

"I remember that there weren't any photographs with the article," she said, looking at her hands to avoid her aunt's eyes. "Couldn't Mark find any pictures of the twins?"

She sensed her aunt's sudden stillness. "Photographs?" Mae repeated. "Um, no, there weren't any photographs available to him."

"So no photos of them survived?"

Aunt Mae hesitated so long that Bailey looked up. She could see her aunt's indecision, and felt a surge of hope. Aunt Mae would never lie to her.

"Well, yes, there is one photograph," Mae answered finally. "I found it in the attic just after Dean and I moved in. Dean didn't want it used in the article—I suppose he was afraid something might happen to it in the process. Or something like that," she added.

Mae had never been good at prevarication.

"I would love to see it," Bailey said, trying to sound casual. "Do you know where Dean keeps it?"

Mae nodded reluctantly.

"It's in his room. You should ask him to show it to you when he and Anna get back."

"I don't think he'd mind if I look at it now, do you?" Bailey asked, standing.

"I don't know, Bailey. It doesn't seem right for you to go rummaging through his things when he's away. Why don't we at least wait for him to call so you can ask his permission?"

"Heavens, Aunt Mae, Dean and I have never been so formal. He knows I won't snoop through his personal stuff. I just want to see the photo. You know how I am about old photographs and other mementos of the past."

Mae twisted her fingers, and the dagger of guilt twisted more deeply into Bailey's stomach. She felt terrible about putting her sweet aunt on the spot like this, but she had to see that photograph. She simply had to.

"All right," Mae said at last. "You can get the key from the front desk. The photograph is in the drawer of the nightstand on the left of the bed. I'm sure you'll find it fascinating. The twins are standing in front of the inn. You'll, er, you'll notice that Anna bears a striking resemblance to her cousins. Strong family genes, I suppose."

"How interesting," Bailey murmured, already moving toward the doorway.

She paused before leaving the room, and turned back to face her aunt. "Aunt Mae—thank you."

Mae nodded, still looking troubled. "Lock up when you leave your brother's room."

"I will."

"And Bailey?"

"Yes?"

"You will tell me why this is so important to you later, won't you?"

"You have my word," Bailey answered sincerely.

Whatever happened, Aunt Mae would know the truth, she decided. The woman had taken in an orphaned little girl and raised her with love and patience and trust. She deserved better than the manipulations Bailey had just put her through.

BAILEY HELD her breath as she set her hand on the brass knob of the Chippendale nightstand in the bedroom Dean and Anna shared. Her hand was shaking so hard she had difficulty opening the drawer.

She saw the framed photograph immediately, but it took her a moment to pick it up. She wasn't sure what, exactly, she hoped to learn from it.

She picked it up slowly. A moment later, she sat heavily on the edge of the bed.

From within the black-and-white photograph, Bran's face swam in her tear-blurred vision. His somber dark eyes were the same, and the arrogant tilt to his chin—even the way he wore his hair, longish on top and back, neat sideburns edging his firm cheeks. He looked no different in this seventy-plus-year-old photograph than when she'd seen him less than an hour ago.

She had only to glance at the woman beside him in the photograph to know that it was Anna. There could be no mistaking the lovely oval face, the glittering dark eyes, the impish, challenging smile.

Family resemblance? No. This was Anna, and Aunt Mae probably knew it—or at least suspected it. No wonder she'd tried to steer Bailey away from the photograph.

One tear escaped her as Bailey touched a trembling fingertip to Bran's pictured face. *Ian's* face, she corrected herself. Ian Cameron—who'd been dead for over seventy-five years.

"Have you found your answers, dear?" Mae asked from the doorway.

Bailey looked up slowly. "Some of them," she whispered. "Not all."

"Are you ready to talk to me?"

Bailey felt another tear fall, as more welled up in her eyes. "I—I have to speak to someone else first," she said. "If I can."

Would she ever see him again? And what would she say if she did?

Why hadn't he told her the truth?

"Some people thought their spirits were freed when the truth about their deaths was revealed," Mae commented, nodding toward the photograph. "But true justice was denied them, you know. Their stepbrother murdered them and then went on to live a long time as a wealthy and prominent citizen of this town. He never had to pay for his crime—not in this life, anyway. I think that's terribly unfair, don't you?"

Bailey nodded, unable to speak.

"I've always believed in second chances," Mae added. "I've wondered if the twins would have theirs. Maybe, I thought, if they could find someone to love them, they could be given another opportunity at life."

If they could find someone to love them. The words seemed to echo in Bailey's mind, as though there was something she should learn from them.

"Bailey?" Mae asked after another moment of silence. "Who is Bran?"

Bailey's fingers tightened convulsively on the wooden frame. She'd almost overlooked Aunt Mae's phenomenal memory, and her disconcerting ability to assemble the slimmest of clues into a startlingly accurate conclusion.

Bailey cleared her throat, but her voice was still rather hoarse. "Bran is . . . a man with too many secrets," she managed to say.

"I see."

"I have to go out now, Aunt Mae," Bailey said abruptly, clutching the photograph to her chest as she stood. "I'll be back inside later to talk to you."

Mae looked resigned. "Dean acted exactly this way when he was falling in love with Anna," she murmured. "Always dashing off without explanation."

"I'm sorry. I—"

"Never mind." Mae waved a dismissing hand. "Do what you have to do, Bailey. I'll lock up here."

"Thank you." Bailey paused to kiss her aunt's cheek on the way out. "I love you, Aunt Mae."

"I love you, too, dear. And I think you deserve a second chance, too. I hope you find it."

Bailey swallowed hard, turned on one heel and made her escape, the old photograph still cradled in her arms.

IT WAS GETTING dark outside. The days were growing so much shorter as winter approached, Bailey mused. The nights so much longer.

It seemed she was destined to spend them alone.

She headed toward the gazebo. She could still recall that first moment when she'd opened her eyes and seen Bran standing there, gazing back at her. She remembered now that he had looked momentarily startled when she'd spoken to him. Apparently, he hadn't expected her to see him.

Would he appear to her now if she waited for him there?

But the gazebo was occupied. A man and a woman snuggled on the bench beneath the festive little lights, oblivious to the world around them.

Honeymooners, Bailey thought with a deep sigh.

Did they have any idea how fortunate they were?

She turned and quietly walked away, suspecting that the couple never heard her footsteps crunching softly on the garden path.

Bran wasn't waiting outside her cottage. As she turned the key in the lock, she wondered if she would find him inside. Locked doors hadn't kept him out before—and she knew now that she *had* locked them.

The cottage was empty.

She closed the door behind her. "Bran?" she called softly. "Are you here?"

Where had he gone when he hadn't been with her? Had he been here all along, silently watching her? Did he see her now? Hear her? "Bran? Please, I need to talk to you."

Nothing.

She sat on the couch and looked at the old photograph in her lap. Her thoughts were a maelstrom of questions, emotions, memories, doubts. Shadows crept like wraiths across the floor as the evening advanced. Bailey hadn't bothered to turn on the lights when she'd come in; the darkness didn't trouble her now. It seemed appropriate for the newest turn her life had taken.

If only she could talk to him. She touched a fingertip to the shadowy face in the photograph and leaned her head wearily against the back of the couch, closing her eyes. She wished there were some way she could contact him.

When she opened her eyes again, he was there.

10

December 7, 1910

Something is wrong with me. I have difficulty explaining, even to Dr. Cochrane, but I know that something is not right. I tire so easily these days. My limbs feel heavy, and there is a weakness in my right hand. Last night, my water glass fell from my fingers, as though all the strength had left my grip. My head seems to hurt all the time. Not excruciating. It is just a constant, dull, nagging ache.

Gaylon is worried. I see it in his eyes when he looks at me. I believe the staff is beginning to worry, as well. They have been so kind, so solicitous lately. Particularly Emma. She frets so. I wish she wouldn't, especially now that she is expecting a baby. Poor Emma. Pregnant and left alone. Gaylon wanted to let her go when she told us. I told him we would do no such thing. Emma Watson has been with me for years. I will not turn my back on her in her time of need. I've promised that she will have a job here at the inn for as long as she needs one.

Gaylon wants me to make a will. He said we both ought to, in case something should happen to one of us. He assured me he doesn't think there is any reason to worry about my health, but he has mentioned the will several times. He told me he wants to provide for Charles, entrusting the boy to my care until he reaches his majority. And, he wishes me to settle the ownership of the inn in case I die before he does.

The inn, of course, belongs to my children. James built this place with his dreams, his sweat, his hopes and his love. There has never been any question in my mind that it will belong to his son and his daughter. I told Gaylon that. He has always agreed with me that I could make no other choice.

He has asked me to name him as executor of the estate until the twins reach their twenty-fifth birthday, should I die before that day. He said it would be best for the inn, and for the twins. He promised he would take care of the place, that he would turn it over at the proper time without hesitation. I have been married to him long enough now to believe in his sincerity. He has enjoyed managing the inn, and he will not look forward to the day it is no longer his to control, but he will honor his promise.

As for Charles, he shows no interest in innkeeping. To be honest, Charles displays little interest in anything other than his books and his lofty dreams of someday having a great deal of money. He knows all too well that he would never make that kind of fortune with this simple country inn. We get by, but we have never been rich. Nor have I ever cared. I have my children. I consider myself wealthy, indeed.

I must consider the possibility that I will die before my children are grown. I must decide what would be best for them. Obviously, they need guidance. Twenty-five does not seem an unreasonable age for them to become responsible for the management of the inn. Mary Anna will most likely marry before then, and move into a new home with her husband, but Ian, I think, will stay on. He loves this inn deeply. He has always expected to own it someday. Gaylon's suggestion has merit.

Gaylon and I will speak to our man of affairs next week. Regardless of my state of health now, these things should not be left to chance. I hope I will be here to watch my children grow to adulthood, to see my daughter married, to hold my grandchildren in my arms. I hope to be the one to pass the ownership of the inn to my son when the time is right. But if I am not granted that much more time, then I want to die knowing that I have done my best for my children.

I love them so much.

BAILEY WASN'T SURE he was really there at first. The room was so dim by now that he was only a darker silhouette against the shadows. And then he moved toward her.

She jumped up and turned on the light.

He looked exactly the same. His hair, his face, the dark shirt and suit. The look of hopeless longing in his eyes.

But she couldn't see him in exactly the same way she had before, she realized dazedly. Where before she'd thought him just an exasperatingly enigmatic man who intrigued her more than any man she'd ever known, now she knew who—and what—he really was. And she was having a great deal of trouble knowing what to do about it. What she felt. How she should act.

"Bran," she whispered, and moistened her lips, which had gone dry and stiff.

"Bailey," he said, searching her face intently. "Are you all right? How long have I been gone?"

Where had he gone? And why?

She cleared her throat, trying to concentrate on his questions rather than her own. "I—I don't know, exactly," she said, having no idea of the time. "A few hours."

She didn't try to answer his first question. She couldn't. She wasn't at all sure she *was* all right.

His gaze fell to the wooden frame she held like a shield against her breasts. "What are you holding?"

Slowly, she turned the photograph toward him.

His eyelashes flickered. "Where did you find that?"

"Dean had it hidden in his room. Aunt Mae told me about it."

"It's a very good picture of Anna," he murmured.

She nodded. "And of you."

His gaze lifted again, his dark eyes flaming so intently she could almost feel the heat. "I didn't know how to tell you."

The first flicker of anger penetrated the numbing shock Bailey had felt since that moment when Elva had looked at Bran and hadn't seen him. "I see. So you left me in ignorance. You lied to me."

He winced. "I never lied to you," he insisted. "I just didn't tell you . . . everything."

"You lied, Bran," she insisted, clinging to the anger. It was so much easier to bear than the grief. "Or should I call you Ian? Or whoever the hell you are."

She lifted an unsteady hand to her aching temple. "God, I feel like Lois Lane," she muttered.

He frowned. "Who?"

"Another woman too stupid to put two and two together and come up with the truth."

"You aren't stupid. Far from it."

"Funny," she said with a flat laugh, "I'm feeling pretty dense. I came here to escape the mess I'd made of my life in Chicago, and now look what I've done. I've fallen for a ghost."

"I told you I didn't want that to happen."

"Didn't you?" she asked, remembering her aunt's theory.

"What do you mean?" he asked, narrowing his eyes.

"Having Dean fall in love with your sister apparently gave her another chance at life. Maybe you thought the same thing would happen for you."

He visibly recoiled. "You can't believe that."

"I don't know what to believe anymore," she whispered. "I only know that I'm so damned tired of being used by the men I meet."

His own temper flared, making his face harden, his eyes glitter dangerously. His voice was very soft. "You're comparing me to that man who threatened you? And the other fools who preceded him?"

"There weren't that many," she snapped defensively. "But they did have one thing in common with you. They didn't mind lying when it suited their purposes, either."

"Bailey." He moved closer, his hand lifted toward her, his expression softened. "Let me explain—"

Instinctively, she flinched.

He froze. His hand clenched, then dropped to his side. The look in his eyes broke her heart.

"I'm sorry," she whispered. "I—"

"The one possibility I couldn't accept," he said hoarsely, "was that you would be afraid of me."

"But I'm—"

A sudden pounding on the door, so hard and so loud it rattled the windows, made Bailey jump.

"Bailey! Bailey, please. Help us!"

The muffled cry was Cara's. Even through the door, the terror in her voice was obvious.

Bailey dropped the photograph and sprang for the door. She fumbled with the locks for a moment. Cara and Casey fell inside almost before Bailey could get the door fully open. Both of them were pale and crying.

"Lock it!" Cara insisted, shoving the door closed. "He's out there. We have to call someone."

Bailey had already turned the lock. "Who's out there?" she demanded. "What's going on?"

Cara put her arms around her whimpering, trembling daughter and huddled over her. "His name is Rance Owens. I testified against him two years ago. He went to prison, but he escaped. He's been looking for me ever since. I don't know how he found me this time, but—oh, Bailey, we have to get help. He's insane. He won't stop until—"

"I'll call the police," Bailey said, snatching up the telephone and listening to the dial tone. "You and Casey sit on the couch. You'll be safe in here." *She hoped.*

She watched as Cara led Casey to the couch, passing within inches of the man who stood there looking at Bailey with concern. It was quite obvious that they weren't aware of his presence.

"Summon the police," he urged. "If he's determined enough, your locks won't keep him out."

Bailey nodded and dialed 911. She waited with held breath for a ring at the other end of the line. She heard only silence.

Praying she'd done something wrong, she pressed the disconnect button, then waited impatiently for another dial tone.

There wasn't one.

"Oh, God," she whispered, trying again for a tone. "Oh, no."

"What's wrong?" Ian demanded.

She looked at him helplessly. "I think he's cut the line. I can't get through to anyone."

"Damn."

Cara gasped. "You can't get through?"

Bailey turned toward the couch. "No. The phone isn't working."

Casey sobbed and hid her face in her mother's chest.

Bailey made a sudden decision. "I'll run for help," she said. "You lock the doors behind me and then lock yourselves into the bathroom. There's no window in there."

"*No!*"

"No, Bailey. You don't know him like I do. He's crazy. He'll do anything to get to me."

Ian and Cara had spoken at the same time. Bailey focused on Cara as she argued. "He isn't after me," she said. "We can't just stay out here waiting for him to make a move. I have to get help. It's only a few yards to the inn. If the phones are out there, I'll get the staff, the guests, anyone I can find to help us."

"Bailey, no," Ian protested. "If he's as dangerous as she says, he won't hesitate to hurt you. I—I can't protect you," he added, obviously hating the admission of impotence.

She looked at him, then, not caring that Cara might find it strange. "I have to do something."

"And if he has a gun?" Ian's expression was tortured now. "I couldn't bear it if you died out there in the darkness, Bailey. The way—"

The way Anna and I did. The words hung unspoken in the air between them.

She swallowed hard. "I—"

Her words were drowned out by the crash of an explosive kick against the front door. Metal grated. Wood groaned. A second kick shattered the doorjamb.

Cara and Casey screamed.

Bailey ran toward them. "In the bedroom!" she cried. At least there would be one more lock Owens would have to go through if he made it past the front door, she thought desperately.

Wood splintered beneath the force of another kick.

"Get out of here, Bailey!" Ian shouted. "Lock the bedroom door, open the window and scream as loudly as you can."

They might have made it to the bedroom if Casey hadn't fallen. Bailey and Cara wasted precious moments hauling the child to her feet.

One more kick and the front door flew open, a mess of broken wood. The man in the doorway was huge. Dark-haired. Red-faced. His eyes were black with rage and what Bailey instantly identified as drug-fueled insanity.

She threw herself between the intruder and the others. She had nothing for a weapon, no lamp, no fireplace poker. Nothing. She really was going to have to talk to her brother about furnishing this place, she thought fleetingly.

Owens glanced at Bailey, curled his lip and jerked his head toward the door. "Get out of here."

"Cara, Casey, get in the bedroom." Bailey moved backward with them, toward the open bedroom doorway.

Casey was screaming. Owens advanced steadily toward them, his massive fists clenched, breathing loud and ragged. "Shut her up," he told Cara. "Or I'm going to have to do it myself."

"Leave them alone," Bailey insisted, trying to shield the child.

"Get out of my way."

"Bailey, run," Ian urged, looking both deadly furious and despairingly powerless. "Go get help."

For only a moment, Bailey considered doing as he said, considering the chances that she could escape and bring help before Owens could hurt either Cara or Casey. But then she looked again at the madness blazing in Rance Owens's eyes as he moved grimly toward Cara, and she knew there wasn't time.

"Leave them alone!" she screamed again. "Get out of here!"

All his concentration focused on Cara, Owens didn't even seem to hear Bailey. She might as well have been as invisible as Ian.

"I've got you now, bitch," he said, the words hissing with ominous satisfaction. "You took everything from me. Everything. And now it's time for you to pay."

He reached out for Cara. Without stopping to think, Bailey threw herself at him, kicking, swinging, clawing.

As though she were little more than an annoying insect, Owens swung a fist at her, connecting solidly with the side of her head—the same side that was still swollen from the accident.

The blow rocked her backward, the pain stunning her, blinding her. She reeled, then crumpled.

"No!" The enraged roar came from Ian.

Bailey thought she felt something—someone—rush past her. And then Owens grunted in surprise. "Where the hell—"

His voice was abruptly choked off.

Bailey heard the sounds of battle as she tried to rise, blinking rapidly to clear her pain-blurred vision. She focused just well enough to see Ian and Owens struggling in the center of the room, both staggering to keep their footing as they grimly fought for dominance.

Cara and Casey knelt beside Bailey. "Bailey, are you all right? Oh, God, you're bleeding," Cara said, on the verge of hysteria.

"Take—take Casey and get out of here," Bailey managed to whisper, her stomach wrenching. "Get help."

Owens's fist connected with Ian's jaw, snapping Ian's head back. Bailey gasped as Ian rocked from the impact. Owens hit him again. A crimson smear of blood stained Ian's mouth.

She pushed herself to her feet, shrugging off Cara's concerned hands. Owens was so much larger than Ian, so dangerous in his dementia. She had to do something to help.

The only weapon she could find was Dean's laptop computer, which she'd left lying on the bar. The six-pound device felt unsatisfactorily light in her hands, but the case was constructed of hard plastic.

She ran up behind Owens and slammed it with all her strength against the back of his head.

Owens faltered. Ian took advantage of the opportunity to drive his fist into the larger man's face.

Owens went down. Hard.

"What the hell? What's going on in here? Cara!" Mark rushed through the splintered doorway. He went straight to Cara and jerked her roughly into his arms. "Are you all right?"

She started to speak, then caught her breath and buried her face in his shoulder. His arms closed protectively around her.

Bailey stared down at Owens. "Is he out?"

"For now," Ian said grimly. He looked at her face. "You're bleeding."

She felt the warm liquid dripping from her temple. It throbbed, as did her sore ankle, which she'd twisted again.

She ignored the discomfort. Her eyes were locked on Ian's mouth. On the blood that oozed from the deep cut at one corner. "You—"

"Bailey, who is this?" Mark demanded, looking down at Owens. He had one arm around Cara, the other around Casey. Both clung to him.

"He was after Cara," Bailey said, dragging her attention from Ian.

Cara drew a deep breath and repeated the explanation she had given Bailey.

"I walked into a convenience store in Tampa just as he shot the clerk," she added. "He fired at me, hit me in the shoulder and thought he had killed me. I lived to testify against him. He warned me then that he would find me and kill me. When I heard he'd escaped from prison, I knew he would come after me. Casey and I got into the car and just started driving. We ended up here. I—I thought we would be safe."

"That's why you were so frightened all the time," Mark murmured. "You were afraid he would find you. Why didn't you tell us?"

"I had a terrible experience with the press in Tampa," she explained quietly. "The reporters seemed to be fascinated with my part in the trial. They hounded me. It was because of them that Owens knew so much about me, even though I begged them to leave me alone. I—I was afraid that if . . . another reporter learned about me, he wouldn't be able to resist the lure of a sensational story."

Mark tilted her remorseful face upward. "You were wrong," he said flatly.

"I know," she whispered. "I think I knew all along that you weren't like that. But I still thought it best for you to stay away from me. I—I didn't want to risk anyone else getting hurt because of me."

She looked at Bailey, her eyes brimming with tears. "I'm so sorry you were hurt again," she said, her voice choked. "Casey and I were in the garden when Owens jumped out at us. This was the closest place for me to run to. I didn't want to involve you, but I was so afraid he would hurt Casey."

"You did the right thing," Bailey assured her firmly. "I'm fine, Cara."

Cara nodded, clearly struggling to reclaim her composure. "Thanks to your friend," she said, turning to Ian with an unsteady smile. "I haven't even had a chance to thank you yet," she told him.

Ian's eyes widened.

Bailey gasped.

Cara could see him.

"I—you're welcome," Ian managed to say, glancing at Bailey in question.

Mark was looking at Ian now, his face creased with a frown. "You look familiar," he murmured. "Have we met?"

"This . . . this is, er, Bran Cameron," Bailey stammered, then decided that further explanation was called for. "Anna's brother."

Mark's jaw dropped. "Anna's *brother?*"

Did Mark know? Bailey wondered, thinking of the times he'd acted so oddly when Anna's name was mentioned.

Ian nodded, watching Mark warily.

Mark closed his mouth. "Well," he said a bit weakly. "Whoever you are, I'm grateful to you for helping Cara and Casey."

Ian cleared his throat and nodded toward the prostrate form at his feet. "We'd better see to him. He'll be coming around soon."

Before Mark could respond, they were interrupted. Belatedly drawn by the noise and commotion from the cottage, others had come to investigate. Sometime during the pandemonium that followed, Bailey realized that Ian was gone.

SHORTLY AFTERWARD, Owens was taken away. Almost excited at having a real live escaped convict in his jurisdiction, Chief Roy Peavy himself supervised the arrest, looking uncharacteristically commanding in his crumpled uniform. Like the others, he suspected that Owens had been involved in the "accident" the night before, and predicted that Owens's prints would be found in the stolen truck.

"He didn't even care if he killed anyone else trying to get to me," Cara whispered with a shudder.

Mark slipped an arm around her shoulder. "He won't bother you again, honey. No one will ever threaten you again."

Her cheeks pink, Cara looked up at him. Bailey felt a lump form in her throat at the look in Cara's eyes. She suspected that Cara had been concealing her true feelings for months, and was just now allowing them to show.

It appeared to Bailey that Mark's patience and perseverance had finally paid off. She was delighted for both of them.

Mae had fussed over Bailey until Bailey had begged her to go rest. The latest excitement had been almost too much for Mae. She had finally allowed Elva to lead her away.

"Cara, you should put Casey to bed," Bailey murmured, nodding toward the little girl who was so drained that she was swaying on her feet. "She's wiped out."

"I know. I just want to thank you again for what you did."

Bailey smiled wearily and squeezed Cara's outstretched hands. "I'm just glad it's all over. You're safe now."

"Yes." Cara looked dazed at the realization. "Safe," she whispered.

"Take Casey on in," Mark urged her. "I'll be there in a few minutes."

And then Mark and Bailey were alone.

"You obviously can't stay here tonight," he commented, nodding toward the broken front door.

"No. I'll sleep in one of the rooms in the inn. I just want to collect some of my things."

Mark touched the lump at the side of her head. "You're sure you're all right? I wish you'd let me take you to the doctor."

"It's just a lump, Mark. I'm getting used to them by now. Really, I appreciate your concern, but I don't want to see another doctor tonight."

He glanced around the trampled room. "What happened to, er, Bran?"

Bailey didn't blink. "He had some things to do."

"Would you like me to wait for you to get your things so I can walk you to the inn?"

"No, thank you. I may take a while to pack. You should go to Cara."

"You don't mind being out here alone now?"

"No." She smiled weakly. "I don't think anyone would dare pester me after all the commotion tonight. And if someone does become a nuisance, I swing a mean computer."

He searched her face, hesitated a moment, then nodded. "All right. But if you're not inside in an hour, I'm coming after you," he warned.

She smiled. "Don't push your luck, Winter."

He returned her smile, and moved toward the doorway. He stopped halfway there and bent to pick something up. When he turned, he was holding the framed photograph in his hand.

Bailey stood very still as Mark looked at the photograph in silence for what seemed like a very long time. She couldn't read his expression.

Finally, he lifted his head. "Here," he said, holding it out to her. "You'd better put this somewhere safe. It looks . . . very old."

She took it from him gratefully. "I will," she whispered. "Thank you, Mark."

He chuckled hollowly. "I'm learning not to ask a lot of questions around here."

Before she could respond, he turned and walked out the shattered door.

BAILEY WANDERED into her bedroom, vaguely intending to pack. She knew the packing had been only an excuse. Truth was, she was waiting for Bran. She still had trouble thinking of him as Ian.

She had to believe he would come back to her. She refused to accept the possibility that he had left her life forever. She could still so clearly picture the look in his eyes when he'd told her that he didn't want her hurt.

He had to care—at least a little, she told herself.

She only hoped she hadn't driven him away with her angry accusations.

She loved him. She didn't know when it had happened, though she suspected it might have been that moment when he'd turned to her after their first meeting and told her she had a lovely smile. Or maybe it had been last night, when he'd awakened her from her nightmare and had so obviously raged against his helplessness to comfort her. She hadn't understood then. Now that she did, her heart twisted in sympathy for him.

Would he, like his sister, be given a second chance to live? And if so, would he want to spend that new life with her? She loved him enough to accept what he was. Whatever he had to give. If only some miracle would grant them the opportunity.

She wanted so much to see him. To talk to him. But she didn't know where to look. She could only wait, and hope that he would come back to her soon.

She stood, deciding she might as well start packing while she waited.

Her suitcase was in the closet, next to the box of old books she still hadn't taken the time to go through. She took out her suitcase, then paused, and looked at the box with a frown. Some impulse she couldn't understand made her set down her suitcase and kneel beside the box.

She dug through the musty volumes inside, giving only cursory glances at the titles and publication dates. She set them in hastily organized piles on the floor, one stack for the ones she knew to be worthless, another for the ones that merited further inspection. She didn't know why it suddenly seemed so important to do this now.

The journal was at the very bottom of the box. Bailey opened the cover, then caught her breath when the name written inside leapt out at her.

Amelia Townsend Cameron Peavy. The name Peavy had obviously been added later, in different ink.

Though the writing was splotched and badly faded, Bailey could make out many of the words. The first entry was dated February 16, 1896. *"My babies are two days old, diary. My twins. Ian and Mary Anna."*

Ian. Mary Anna. Bailey sank onto her heels, her breath caught in her throat. This journal had been written by Ian's mother, over one hundred years ago.

It was almost too much for Bailey to take in.

She kept reading.

They were his final gift to me—born on Valentine's Day. And though I know it sounds foolish, I made a special wish for them on the night they were born. I prayed that they would not leave this earth without finding the love my darling James and I were fortunate enough to share. I wished that they would each meet someone who would love them absolutely, and that they would feel that same unconditional love in their own hearts. Would that I had the power to grant my own request for them.

"Oh, my God," Bailey whispered, looking from the diary to the old photograph she'd left on the nightstand.

She had accused Ian of using her. Of manipulating her to fall in love with him so that he could come back to life. But that hadn't been what his mother had wished for him. She had wanted him to be loved—and to know true love in return.

She remembered again the way he'd looked at her. The undeniable pain in his face when she'd unintentionally flinched away from him. The helpless rage he'd expressed when her safety had been threatened.

Mark and Cara and the others had seen him. Heard him. Felt him.

And there had been blood on his mouth.

A wave of hope swept through her, making her hands tremble. She forced her attention back to the journal, hungry to learn all she could about Ian's former life.

11

September 18, 1911

It is becoming harder to pretend to the children that I will recover. We have been telling them that Mama just doesn't feel well. We have led them to believe that I need only rest and time. I can't bring myself to tell them what I now know to be true.

Ian suspects, I think. He has become so quiet during the past months. So withdrawn. Perhaps he is preparing himself for the separation he dreads. I do not believe he has shared his fears with his sister. She seems as happy as ever. She waits on me so sweetly, as though her tender care will hasten my recovery. My poor darlings.

Emma has been a godsend. She gives my children so much love and attention, and is still such a wonderful mother to her own little Billy. What would I do without her now?

I haven't the strength to write any more now. The children will be home from school soon. I want to be able to greet them with smiles and hugs. There is so little time left for me to be with them.

BAILEY'S FACE was wet with tears when she sensed his presence in the bedroom doorway. She looked up from the diary that she'd almost finished reading to find him watching her, his black hair disheveled, his lower lip slightly swollen, his dark eyes guarded, watchful.

"Where have you been?" she asked, her voice husky.

"Walking in the woods," he answered. "It's cold out. There's a scent of winter in the air. I scratched my hand on a broken fence post."

More tears escaped her in response to the wonder in his voice. Cold. Fragrance. Pain. Sensations she'd taken for granted for so long.

She never would again.

"Did you enjoy it?" she asked with a tremulous smile.

He didn't smile in return. "No. You weren't there to share it with me."

Her eyes welled again.

"You're crying."

She mopped at her face and nodded. "I've been reading your mother's diary. I hope you don't mind."

He stilled. "My mother's diary?"

She nodded again. "I found it in this box of old books. Oh, Bran—Ian. She was a very special woman. She loved you so much."

He moved slowly toward her, his gaze fixed on the slim volume in her hands. "I didn't know it existed. I never saw it."

"She wrote in it at night mostly, when you and your sister were sleeping. She poured her heart out in these pages."

He knelt beside her. With a reverence that almost made her start crying again, he reached out to touch the journal. "Anna will want to see this."

"Of course. We'll show it to her as soon as she returns."

He lifted his gaze to hers, his eyes still carefully shuttered. "Will we?"

"Yes," she whispered. She drew a deep breath. "About what I said earlier—"

He winced. "It wasn't true, Bailey. I wasn't trying to use you. I only wanted to help you."

"I know that now."

"I didn't try to make you . . . fall in love with me," he continued doggedly. "I tried to keep my distance from you. I knew you deserved better, even if there was a chance that we—"

"Ian, I love you."

His mouth tightened. "I don't need your charity, Bailey," he snapped. "I'm not another of those needy men who used you before. I won't be dependent on your compassion and your assistance."

She thought of the words in his mother's diary. The wish. She looked again at the raw cut on his lip. "It's different this time," she murmured. "I love you. And, oh, Ian, I need you."

His voice was hoarse now. "You deserve better. I have nothing to offer you. I don't belong in your time. I have no job, no skills. I don't know how to use that computer device, or . . . or who Lois Lane is."

Her soft heart twisted, but she held his gaze steadily. "Do you love me?"

"Bailey—"

"Ian," she broke in firmly, clinging to the words in the diary. "Do you love me?"

His eyes were tortured. "Enough to die again if you ask me to," he murmured.

She'd shed more tears in the past hour than she had in months. It seemed she still had more to spare. "Oh, Ian."

She reached out to touch his face. For a moment, it appeared that he would move away from her again. But he stayed where he was, seeming to hold his breath.

She laid her hand gently against the side of his face.

His cheek was firm beneath her fingertips. Warm. The faintest hint of stubble tickled her skin. She felt the muscle work in his jaw as he swallowed.

"I love you," she whispered.

He caught her hand in his own, gripping it so tightly he was in danger of pulverizing her fingers. She didn't protest. He dragged her hand to his mouth, and kissed it. "I love you," he said. "I loved you before I ever met you."

She rubbed her thumb carefully over his battered lower lip. "You haven't even kissed me."

He smiled against her touch. "I know."

"Don't you want to?"

He reached out to move a strand of hair away from her cheek. She felt the tremor in his fingers. "It's been a very long time since I've kissed anyone. What if I've forgotten how?"

She thought she'd explode if he didn't kiss her soon. "It'll come back to you," she assured him, and swayed toward him.

He crushed her against his chest. His mouth covered hers. Bailey threw her arms around his neck, delighted to discover that he hadn't forgotten anything.

The kiss lasted a very long time. Ian finally raised his head, laughing softly and gasping for breath. "Air," he murmured, filling his lungs.

She smiled and touched the cut on his lip. "Doesn't that hurt?"

"Yes. It feels good."

She understood. There were so many questions she wanted to ask him, so much she wanted to understand about the existence he'd led for the past seventy-five years, about Dean and Anna... everything. But that could wait.

She tugged his head toward her and kissed him again.

"Bailey," Ian muttered some time later, dragging his mouth away from hers. His breathing was ragged now, his dark eyes burning with desire. "We should stop. I can't—I want—"

"Make love with me, Ian."

He caught his breath. "You're—you're sure?"

"I want you. Does that shock you?" she asked, belatedly remembering the time he'd lived in before.

He smiled and cupped her face in one large, strong hand. "No," he murmured. "It delights me. I love your honesty. And your courage," he said, brushing his mouth against her.

"Your kindness," he added, kissing her again. "Your loyalty."

She melted into him, hopelessly enthralled by this charmingly seductive side of him.

"Your legs," he said, smiling against her lips. "I particularly like your legs."

She giggled. "If I start listing parts of you that I find especially attractive, I'll really shock you."

His grin was delectably wicked. "We'll have to put that to the test. Later."

They were still kneeling on the floor, beside the stacks of books. Ian stood and reached down a hand to her.

Bailey's legs, folded into the same position for so long, protested when she tried to rise, as did her swollen ankle. She stumbled. Gasping, she clutched at him for balance.

Ian promptly swung her into his arms, high against his chest. "Do you have any idea," he asked huskily, "how badly I've wanted to carry you to bed?"

"I know how badly I've wanted you to," she answered candidly. "But, er, what about the front door? We can't lock it. We can't even close it."

He kicked the bedroom door shut. "We can lock this one. Where's the key?"

She reached down to depress the lock button. "It's locked."

He glanced at it doubtfully for a moment, then shrugged, making her cling more tightly to him. And then he strode toward the bed.

BAILEY WAS utterly fascinated by Ian's body. Only one word came to her mind to describe it. *Perfection*.

Kneeling beside him, she ran her hands down his warm, sleek chest. Her fingertips glided over brown nipples, well-defined muscles, his flat, hard stomach. "You're so beautiful," she breathed.

He lay on his back, his hands sliding upward to cup her breasts. "No. You're the beautiful one."

She leaned over to kiss him, tracing his firm lips with the tip of her tongue, and then shivered when his thumbs rotated lazily against her hardened nipples. "I . . . don't think you have to worry about whether you've forgotten anything," she managed to say as she sank onto him. "You haven't."

He rolled, pinning her beneath him. "We should make sure, don't you think?"

He was hard and hot against her thigh, letting her know just how badly he wanted her. She arched against him. "Show me," she demanded.

He kissed her deeply. Lingeringly. And then he moved lower, tasting her cheek, her jaw, her throat. Her breasts. She buried her fingers in his luxuriant dark hair, her eyes closing, her pulse racing. When his mouth moved lower still, she gasped and arched upward, her heels digging into the soft sheets.

If there was anything he'd forgotten, he proved very talented at improvising.

"Please," she gasped, tugging at his hair. "I need you."

He gathered her close. "I need you, too," he admitted. "I've never needed anyone like this before."

"I love you."

"I love you," he repeated, holding her eyes with his own as he slid slowly, deeply into her. "Forever, Bailey."

She wrapped her legs around his hips, holding him tightly. "Forever," she whispered. And then he began to move, and the power of speech left her completely.

SOME TIME LATER, Ian cradled Bailey against his heart and reflected that he had wasted much of his first twenty-five years on earth. He had never known what it was to truly live . . . until tonight.

Making love with Bailey had been like nothing he'd ever known before. True, his experiences had been rather limited, but he had no regrets about that. He'd been waiting for Bailey to show him what it was like to love. To be loved.

"This is what she meant," he murmured.

Bailey lifted her head. "What who meant?" she asked drowsily.

"My mother. I told her once that I didn't understand all the fuss about romance, why so many people seemed obsessed with it when there were so many more important things to think of. She just smiled and said that someday I would understand that there is nothing more important than love. Nothing in this life—or beyond."

"She must have been thinking of your father when she said that," Bailey murmured. "She loved him so much. She never really got over his death."

"I know. She taught us to love him, too, even though we never had the chance to meet him."

"She gave you this, you know."

"What?"

"This." Her hand pressed against his chest, over his steadily beating heart. "The night you were born, she made a wish that you wouldn't leave the earth without finding love. I think that's why you're still here. Why you—and Anna—have been given a second chance."

"Anna was waiting for Dean and I—I was waiting for you," he murmured, struck by the possibility that she was right.

Her eyes glowed. "Yes," she said with some satisfaction. "You were waiting for me."

He drew her closer. "I couldn't have asked for a more precious gift."

She tugged his head down to hers.

They both jumped when someone knocked loudly on the bedroom door. "Bailey?" Mark called out from the other side. "Hey, Bailey, are you in there? Are you all right?"

She groaned. "I'm fine, Mark. Go away."

"C'mon, Bailey, you can't stay out here by yourself. We're all worried about you. Come into the inn with me, okay?"

"She's fine, Mark," Ian called out on a quick, devilish impulse. "Go away."

There was a sudden silence outside the door. And then the sound of a throat being loudly cleared. "Yeah, okay. Er, sure. I'll, uh, see you tomorrow, right?"

"Good night, Mark," Bailey said. Then she dissolved into giggles as he made a noisy and rapid exit from the cottage.

"You," she told Ian with a mock scowl, "are bad."

"So I've been told. Did I embarrass you?"

"Are you kidding? You've ruined my reputation. You know what you'll have to do now, don't you?"

"Make love to you again," he said promptly.

She threw her arms around his neck. "That'll work."

IT WAS ALMOST DAWN when Bailey woke. There was just enough light in the room for her to see Ian, standing by the window, looking out. He wore only his slacks, and his arms were crossed over his chest, as if he was cold. He looked to be very deeply wrapped up in his own thoughts.

Bailey slipped out of bed and walked toward him, wondering what was bothering him. What she could do to help.

He turned at her movement. He stood very still as she approached.

"Ian?" she asked, reaching out to touch his arm. "Are you all right?"

He let out a long, deep breath. "You'll think I'm being foolish."

"No. Tell me."

"I was afraid you'd wake up . . . and you wouldn't see me," he admitted, his voice rough. "That I would reach for you . . . and you wouldn't even know I was here."

There were those pesky tears again. She blinked them furiously away and forced herself to smile as she stepped into his arms. "You won't get away from me that easily, Ian Cameron," she murmured. "I've brought you back, and I'm going to keep you."

His arms locked around her, almost driving the breath from her lungs. "Bailey," he said hoarsely, hiding his face in her hair. "I love you."

She held him tightly. "I love you, too, Ian. Forever."

WARM WATER CASCADED over Ian's shoulders, slid down his chest and arms. Bailey followed one drop from his neck to his navel, marveling at everything she saw between. "I won't ever get tired of looking at you," she murmured. "I've never seen anyone more perfectly formed."

Her compliment seemed to embarrass him. His cheeks reddened from more than the steamy water coming out of the shower head. He muttered something incoherent and very male.

Bailey smiled, testing his right bicep with appreciation. "Nice," she purred.

He growled and looked down at her hand. Then went still. "I had a scar there."

She lifted an inquiring eyebrow. "A scar? Where?"

"Here." His left forefinger traced a path along his right arm, from his elbow almost down to his wrist. "I ripped my arm open on a sheet of jagged metal. Ol' Doc Cochrane had to sew it back up. It left a scar."

She studied his flawless skin. "It isn't there now."

Ian lifted his right knee. "There was another scar here," he said, pointing to his kneecap. "I fell on a piece of glass while playing tag with Anna."

"You were an accident-prone child, weren't you? But I don't see any scars, Ian."

He shook his head, leaning back against the tiled wall. "I don't understand any of this."

"Maybe we aren't supposed to understand. Let's just be grateful."

He touched her face. "I am grateful. For you."

She smiled and kissed his palm. "Good. Don't ever change your mind."

"Never."

"You are going to marry me, aren't you?"

He sighed. "Is it the women who propose marriage in your time, Bailey?"

"*Our* time now," she reminded him. "And, yeah, sometimes they do. When they get tired of waiting for the men to get around to it."

"You'll have to teach me more about your rules," he said lightly enough, but his eyes were troubled.

She searched his face. "You're not going to turn out to be a male chauvinist or anything, are you, Ian? Because I warn you, if you expect me to be some mealymouthed 'little woman,' I'm going to have to disappoint you."

"I don't understand half of what you just said, but I think I get the gist of it. I don't expect you to be mealymouthed, Bailey. I've always admired your candor. But I'm still loath to be wholly dependent on you. I want to learn about your world. To make my own way."

"Then you will," she said steadily. "What do you want to do, Bran? Oh, sorry. I mean Ian."

"Maybe you should keep calling me Bran. It'll save a lot of uncomfortable questions. As for what I want to do, I'm an innkeeper," he answered simply. "I always have been. But this inn isn't mine now—to be honest, it never was. What do you think about finding a new place with me?"

"An inn?" She bit her lip, intrigued. "With your experience at managing an inn, and mine with antiques and computer bookkeeping, we should be able to make a go of it," she murmured.

"Does that mean yes?"

She smiled and pressed her wet body to his. "Yes," she said. "But let's find a place where we won't be in competition with Dean and Anna. Just to keep harmony in the family."

"Good idea." He quickly lost interest in business.

A few moments later, Bailey decided breathlessly that Ian was the one with the truly spectacular ideas.

"BAILEY?" Ian murmured later as she clung to him in the now-cool shower, gasping for breath.

"Mmm?"

"I'll marry you."

She smiled. "I know."

BAILEY HAD JUST finished tying her sneakers when she heard a knock from the front of the cottage.

"Bailey? Bailey, are you in there? Damn, this place is a mess."

Bailey stood with a gasp. "That's Dean!"

Ian paused with one hand at the top button of his shirt. His dark eyes flared with a mixture of anxiety and anticipation. "They're home," he murmured.

Bailey was already halfway across the room. She unlocked the bedroom door and threw it open. "Dean!" she said, finding her brother standing in the mangled outer doorway. "What are you doing here? You aren't supposed to be back for another week."

"Anna had a feeling that we should come back early," he said, scowlingly studying the vandalism of his newly finished cottage. "Looks like she was right. Aunt Mae and Cara just told us what happened while we were gone."

Bailey stepped into his arms for a hug. "There are a few more things you need to hear," she warned him.

He groaned. "I was afraid of that."

"Oh, this is even worse than I imagined," Anna wailed, stepping into the cottage and surveying the mess with appalled eyes. "I wish I'd been here when that terrible man showed up. I'd have given him a piece of my mind."

"Why in the world did you stay out here alone last night?" Dean asked, looking at Bailey in bewilderment. "Aunt Mae and Cara couldn't understand why you wouldn't take a room in the inn."

So Mark hadn't told them that she hadn't been alone.

Bailey cleared her throat. "I, er, didn't spend the night by myself," she explained. "Someone was with me."

Looking bewildered, Dean frowned. "Someone? Who?"

"Congratulate me, Dean. I'm in love."

He sighed, and appeared to brace himself for the worst. "Okay, who is he?" he said. "Really, Bailey, I hope it's not another—"

Anna cut him off with a choked cry.

Knowing what Anna must have seen, Bailey turned toward the bedroom door.

Ian stood there looking at his sister. His dark hair tumbled over his forehead. His dark clothing was wrinkled. There was a bruise at the corner of his mouth.

Bailey thought he had never looked more handsome.

Anna must have agreed. She covered her mouth with her hands, and her eyes filled with tears. "Ian?" she whispered.

He took a step toward her. "Hello, Anna."

"Oh, my God." She threw herself at him. Her hands were all over him as she feverishly convinced herself that he was real, that he was here, that he was alive.

"Oh, my God," she kept saying, over and over. "Ian!"

He pulled her into his arms and hid his face in her hair, the same glossy dark color as his own.

Her own eyes damp again, Bailey leaned her head against her brother's shoulder.

"Well, I'll be damned," Dean breathed. "He's come back."

"For me," Bailey told him with a beaming smile. "I love him, Dean. And he loves me, too."

Dean shook his head. "I never even imagined—"

"There were some things you neglected to tell me about your wife, weren't there?" she asked him a bit too sweetly. "Can you imagine what I've been through for the past couple weeks?"

"Oh, yeah," he said fervently. "Trust me, I understand. If I'd had any idea that you and he—" He shook his head. "I don't know why I'm so surprised. I should know by now that there are no rules."

Bailey laughed softly. "That's what I've decided. Isn't it wonderful?"

Dean looked at his wife's glowing face. "You won't ever hear me complain."

Anna flew across the room and threw her arms around Dean's neck. "It's Ian!" she said. "Dean, it's Ian. And he's alive!"

Dean laughed and hugged her. "I know, darling." Tucking her into his left arm, he held out his right hand to Ian. "It's good to finally see you."

Ian took his hand warmly. "It's good to be seen." He released Dean's hand and pulled Bailey to his side. "I hope you don't mind, but I'm going to marry your sister."

"I don't mind. We should definitely keep this in the family, I think."

Anna clapped her hands in delight. "You're getting married? Ian, you're in love with Bailey?"

There could have been no misinterpreting the smile Ian gave Bailey. Her knees almost melted with the sheer beauty of it. She clung to his arm.

"I love her," he said deeply.

"And I love him," Bailey asserted, her voice trembling.

"Mother was right," Anna whispered. "We both found true love. Charles couldn't keep us from it."

"Bailey found our mother's diary, Anna," Ian told her. "We'll read it together, shall we?"

"Oh, man," Dean muttered, running a hand through his hair. "I don't even want to think about when our kids want us to help them draw a family tree."

Anna laughed. "Remember our pact, darling. We don't dwell on the past, and we don't worry about the future. We savor the present."

He smiled and kissed her. "I forgot. You'll have to remind me occasionally."

"Gladly."

"Looks like I'm going to have to contact those disreputable acquaintances again," Mark Winter commented as he strolled through the front doorway, his deceptively lazy green eyes focused on Ian. "In need of more forged papers, Dean?"

"Most likely," Dean agreed with a crooked smile. He shook Mark's hand. "What are you doing here so early?"

Mark looked a bit dazed. "I stopped by to ask Cara out for a date."

Dean sighed. "Again?"

"Yeah. And, Dean? This time, she accepted."

Dean laughed and cuffed his friend's shoulder.

Bailey smiled up at Ian. He covered the smile with his lips.

Forgetting the others, Bailey kissed him back, thinking happily of love and miracles and very special wishes. And knowing that her own had just been granted.

February 14, 1912

I was able to have dinner with the family this evening, to celebrate the children's birthday. Gaylon carried me to the table. I'm grateful to him for the excellent care he has given me these past difficult months. I know Charles resents the time his father spends with me.

Ian and Mary Anna are sixteen. Almost grown now. I am thankful that I had this much time with them, though I will not be with them much longer. I grow weaker by the day. Even sitting at the dinner table for an hour has exhausted me.

I can't write long, and my handwriting is growing illegible. Yet I want to complete this one last entry. Someday, my children will read these words, and I want them to know that my last days were not unhappy ones. That my last thoughts were of them.

James came to me in my dreams last night. I told him how reluctant I am to leave our children. They still need me so much. I want to know that they will be happy. James told me that he was very proud of me for the way I've raised them. That he knows I have done my best for them. Even my marriage to Gaylon—he understood that I thought it was best for the twins. At least they will have someone to guide them during the remainder of their youth. I won't be leaving them alone.

James assured me that I needn't worry. Our children will be fine, he said. They will each find love. Precious, lasting, lifelong love that will bring them great joy and many years of happiness. James laughed when he told me that their love will come to them in a way that I could not even understand now. It was so good to hear his laughter again.

He is waiting for me. He told me that he grows impatient for me to join him. Now that I know our children will be happy, I find myself eager to go. I've missed James so desperately. Being with him again is all I could ask for myself now.

I'm very tired. I shall close now. I don't expect to write again. Ian, Mary Anna, if someday you find this book and read my words, know that I love you. That I have always loved you. That I always will. Tell your children about me. Love them as I have loved you.

Be happy, my darlings. Someday we will be together again.

With all my love,
Mother.

Women throughout time have
lost their hearts to:

Starting in January 1996, Harlequin Temptation
will introduce you to five irresistible, sexy rogues.
Rogues who have carved out their place in history,
but whose true destinies lie in the arms of
contemporary women.

#569 *The Cowboy*, Kristine Rolofson
(January 1996)

#577 *The Pirate*, Kate Hoffmann
(March 1996)

#585 *The Outlaw*, JoAnn Ross
(May 1996)

#593 *The Knight*, Sandy Steen
(July 1996)

#601 *The Highwayman*, Madeline Harper
(September 1996)

Dangerous to love, impossible to resist!

Take 4 bestselling love stories FREE

Plus get a FREE surprise gift!

BRIDE'S BAY RESORT

UNLOCK THE DOOR TO GREAT ROMANCE AT BRIDE'S BAY RESORT

Join Harlequin's new across-the-lines series, set in an exclusive hotel on an island off the coast of South Carolina.

Seven of your favorite authors will bring you exciting stories about fascinating heroes and heroines discovering love at Bride's Bay Resort.

Look for these fabulous stories coming to a store near you beginning in January 1996.

Harlequin American Romance #613 in January
Matchmaking Baby by Cathy Gillen Thacker

Harlequin Presents #1794 in February
Indiscretions by Robyn Donald

Harlequin Intrigue #362 in March
Love and Lies by Dawn Stewardson

Harlequin Romance #3404 in April
Make Believe Engagement by Day Leclaire

Harlequin Temptation #588 in May
Stranger in the Night by Roseanne Williams

Harlequin Superromance #695 in June
Married to a Stranger by Connie Bennett

Harlequin Historicals #324 in July
Dulcie's Gift by Ruth Langan

Visit Bride's Bay Resort each month wherever Harlequin books are sold.

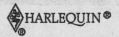

HARLEQUIN ®

If you are looking for more titles by

GINA WILKINS

Don't miss these fabulous stories by one of
Harlequin's most distinguished authors:

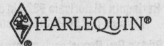

Weddings by DeWilde

Since the turn of the century the elegant and fashionable
DeWilde stores have helped brides around the world
turn the fantasy of their "Special Day" into reality. But now the
store and three generations of family are torn apart by the
separation of Grace and Jeffrey DeWilde. Family members
face new challenges and loves in this fast-paced, glamorous,
internationally set series. For weddings and romance, glamour
and fun-filled entertainment, enter the world of DeWildes...

Watch for WILDE HEART
by Daphne Clair
Coming to you in July 1996

New Zealand TV reporter Natasha Pallas required access to
the famed DeWilde jewel collection at any cost. An upcoming
display at the new Australian store was her best chance, but
how to gain the trust of store manager, Ryder Blake, without
arousing suspicion? Perhaps the distraction of a romance...

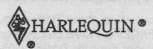

HARLEQUIN ®

Look us up on-line at: http://www.romance.net

WBD4

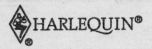